CRYSTAL COVE INN

AIDA EVERHART

CRYSTAL COVE INN

iUniverse books may be ordered through booksellers or by contacting:

iUniverse
1663 Liberty Drive
Bloomington, IN 47403
www.iuniverse.com
1-800-Authors (1-800-288-4677)

Because of the dynamic nature of the Internet, any web addresses or links contained in this book may have changed since publication and may no longer be valid. The views expressed in this work are solely those of the author and do not necessarily reflect the views of the publisher, and the publisher hereby disclaims any responsibility for them.

Any people depicted in stock imagery provided by Getty Images are models, and such images are being used for illustrative purposes only. Certain stock imagery © Getty Images.

ISBN: 978-1-5320-4265-2 (sc)
ISBN: 978-1-5320-4264-5 (e)

Library of Congress Control Number: 2018902004

Print information available on the last page.

iUniverse rev. date: 03/07/2018

CHAPTER 1

THE BEGINNING BOY MEETS GIRL

The early summer climate along the coastline of Puget Sound in Everett, Washington could be some of the most spectacular weather in the Northwest. Blue cloudless skies, a gentle breeze of salty air of the ocean, the subtle Christmas tree scent of the pine trees and the warmth of the sun makes you take a moment to appreciate what Mother Nature has to offer. One Saturday morning, a ray of sunshine peeking through the sheer curtains descended upon a young woman's face as she lay on her bed. The annoying sound of a grumbling diesel truck coming through her bedroom window awakened her. The annoying sound persisted, echoing even louder and closer than before. Unable to go back to sleep, she walked up towards the window to see what was happening. When she partially lifted the curtains, she saw a moving van backing into the unit below her apartment. The movers began to unload the items from the van into the driveway. As she continued to look out her window, the warmth of the sun descended upon her face whiles the gentle breeze from the ocean seemingly brushing against her face. She stood there for a few minutes as she closed her eyes while she took several breaths of fresh air.

For Christina Jensen, most people called her Chris, born and raised in Everett, Washington, a twenty-eight year old, single woman residing in a large apartment complex just a few miles from the beach, moving in or out of the complex is a typical occurrence especially on a Saturday.

Fully awake and an avid runner, she decided to go for a run along the coastline of Puget Sound to avoid all the goings-on below her apartment. It did not take her long to be suited up and put on her running shoes. She remembered having to stop by the apartment manager's office to drop off some fliers for an upcoming "Meet-N-Greet" event for all the occupants in the apartment complex. The leaflet is an invitation to attend an event sponsored by the apartment management to welcome both current and new tenants to meet and greet their neighbor, as well as meeting some of the maintenance staff. You never know when one would need a repairman, plumber or someone that can let you in your apartment in case you accidentally lock yourself out.

Anxious to get going, she hurriedly down the stairs closest to her unit, only to stop in her tracks when she saw a bunch of empty boxes blocking the stairway. She turned around to take the alternate stairway on the opposite side of the building to get down to the ground floor. When she reached the office of the apartment manager, a tall, good-looking man in his early thirties opened the door for her. He had a handful of papers in one hand and a man's bag with a set of keys in the other. Despite the awkwardness of not having a free hand, he managed to be chivalrous and opened the door for Christina. He smiled and slightly nodded his head to acknowledge her presence. She looked his way for a few seconds, just long enough to notice his piercing blue eyes and a dimple on his right cheek, then, quickly look away after she thanked him. He saw her sharp reaction, barely hearing the words "thank you." Perhaps, she may have been in a hurry, or not into talking to strangers. He held the door until she was entirely inside before he went on his way. The apartment manager greeted Chris as she walked in.

"Hi, Chris, you just missed your new neighbor that will be moving in below your unit. I would have made the introductions if you had been here ten seconds earlier. He is a newcomer to the state of Washington and does not have family or friends in the state. Would you kindly introduce yourself and make him feel welcome to the neighborhood. It is a beautiful day for running." the manager commented

"Good morning, Mr. Henderson, I just came by to drop off the fliers for the 'Meet-N-Greet' event. I will make sure I give him a copy of the flier," Chris said.

"Well, thank you, for the fliers; have a good run." Mr. Henderson said

Chris went on her run along the coastline. When she came back to the apartment complex, she saw more empty boxes at the foot of the stairs, further blocking the stairs and the walkway. Somewhat annoyed, she walked over to the other end of the building to take the stairs up to her apartment.

Having just gone for a run and taken a nice, long bath, she took her leisurely time getting ready to do her errands. She fixed herself a cup of tea and brought her tea by the living room window to watch the movers unload the truck. When she finished her tea, she picked up her purse and keys to run some errands. She stepped outside her door and saw the boxes at the foot of the stairs. Much to her dismay, she had to take the long route to her parking stall that would usually take about fifteen steps from the bottom of the stairways. How inconsiderate of this new tenant to be blocking the stairwell, not to mention violating the law on blocking shared access in case of emergency. If they continued to block the stairs by the time she returns, she would have no other choice but to ask the new neighbor to remove the boxes immediately.

She completed her errands and went shopping for about four hours, making the last stop at the grocery store before heading home. By the time she got out of the car, she had a full bag of groceries in one arm and two department bags on the other. She proceeded to take the stairs closest to her unit, thinking that if the empty boxes were still there, she has no other option but to confront the situation. Ready to read the right act to her new neighbor, she did not care what they thought of her. The thought of having to carry her bags all the way around the building, sent the blood rushing to her head. Nonetheless, she approached the stairway closest to her unit to check-out the situation with the boxes. Surprisingly, as she came around the corner to the stairway, all the boxes were gone. When she got to the foot of the stairs, something under the stairwell startled her. She dropped her keys, and the bag of groceries landed on the steps. Luckily, none were breakable. A man sweeping underneath the stairwell picked up the keys and came out from under the stairs to hand the keys to her. He hurriedly picked up the other items that had fallen on the steps. Chris quickly picked up the department store bags making sure that none of the personal items fell out from the bags. She recognized him as the man she ran into that morning at the manager's office.

"Goodness, I did not expect to see anyone there," Chris declared.

"I am sorry, ma'am. I did not mean to startle you," he said apologetically.

He handed Chris the keys and continued to assist her with the other bags. Mark continued his apology.

"I didn't know the movers placed the empty boxes by the stairways. It was not until I came out to empty the trash and saw the stairs filled with boxes. That was not a nice thing to do, so I am truly sorry. I would like to make it up to you, just name my reparation, and I shall obey. By the way, my name is Mark Ingram."

"Hello, Mark Ingram. My name is Christina Jensen, but you can call me Chris. I have the unit right above yours. I saw you this morning at the manager's office. Welcome to you and your family!" Chris extended her hand for the handshake and to receive her keys.

"Thank you; I would be the only one moving into the apartment. I am new to this area, actually to the entire Pacific Coast region. This is my first trip out here. After having lived in Europe for five years and enjoyed every minute of my stay, I also wanted to get back to U.S.A, so here I am. May I help you with your bags?" he politely asked

"You did very well picking up my items. I should be able to handle it from here." Chris said

"One last thing, I like to pay for dinner for the entire family as my peace offering for blocking the stairway. It would make me feel better, even if it's over a cup of coffee and dessert at your famous Starbucks." Mark insisted

"That would not be necessary, but I will keep it in mind. I should let you go on with your busy moving day. Again, welcome to Everett, Washington" Chris responded

Mark continued cleaning up his area while he quickly glanced at Chris closing her door. He thought about his first impression of her varied from being shy, not liking to talk to strangers to having a jealous husband or boyfriend nearby that may be prohibiting her to interact with another man. He saw something in her eyes that completely contradicts the cold attitude she displayed. Having met her up close, she looked even more beautiful than he remembered from their earlier encounter. He concluded that she must be married or sharing the apartment with a boyfriend. That would be a logical explanation for her demeanor.

The following weeks Mark and Chris saw each other from a distance in the parking garage or around the apartment complex. They would acknowledge each other by a hand wave or a nod. All the time they saw each other, never once did Mark see anyone with her. He can only make out one distinct light footstep from Chris' unit. He could not be sure that Chris lives alone upstairs. He does not recall Chris mentioning having a significant other living with her. He just assumed a good looking gal like her might have a partner. There are several military bases surround the town of Everett. Her partner could be abroad serving in the military service. He assumed that would be the case, so he kept his distance and respected her privacy.

Since their first meeting at the foot of the stairs, Chris could not be more pleased with her new neighbor. Remembering his piercing blue eyes and a cute dimple on his face, she could not forget how attractive he looked. His voice sounded manly, yet, the tone expressed kindness. He had the look of a rugged man, but easy on the eyes and more importantly, a sense of gentleness in his demeanor. For a moment, Chris caught herself thinking about Mark in a pleasant light, despite her strong determination not to have another relationship in a long time. This must have been a fluke thought that came to mind.

In just a few weeks, she noticed the distinct difference between the young couple that previously lived downstairs and the new tenant. Gone are loud music, late night parties and sometimes finding other young people lay out asleep by the stairs. Living alone upstairs, this became alarming to her. Other tenants have complained about the young couple until they were evicted from the apartment complex. Some of the neighbors noticed the big difference and commented to Chris how delighted she must be with her new neighbor. The couple next door to Mark baked a welcome casserole for him and mentioned to Chris what a gentleman and respectful he has been since they first met him. Mark received high marks from the neighbors around him. So far, Mark fixed a flat tire, restarted dead car batteries and helped rescue a cat from a tree. He quickly became popular amongst his neighbors.

One evening just before 7:00 PM Chris went for her run along the coastline and she was on her way back from the run when she ran into Mark on his way to the trash bins.

"Hi, neighbor, did you have a nice run?" Mark waved at Chris.

"Yes, I did. The ocean air was refreshing. How are you? Are you all moved in?" Chris replied, stopping to have a quick chat with Mark.

"I just emptied the last box. Now, it is a matter of putting things away, other than in the living room. Well, enough about my moving adventure. Is this a routine for you to go for a run?" Mark asked

"Yes, it is, but I think I need to be more consistent with it. Running helps me unwind after a long day at work." Chris replied

"Do you normally run by yourself?" Mark asked. His curiosity about Chris intrigues him to ask the question.

"If you are trying to find out if I live alone or not, you probably figured out that I live alone." Chris quickly responded

"Ah shucks, I have been found out. You seem to bring out my bad manners without even trying. What do I need to do to change that?" Mark commented with humor to get a reaction from Chris.

Mark sense of humor by his comment made Chris almost laugh. Chris let out a smile which she tried to hide from him by quickly looking away. However, he could not believe how lovely she looked at that moment with a cute smile on her face that he has not seen before. He thought about not commenting on what just happened, but he could not pass up the opportunity to tell her how sweet she looked to see a friendly face.

"Wow, did I just see a smile from you?" Mark commented, trying to get more reaction from Chris.

"I should let you go on with what you were doing. Have a good evening." Chris was just about to leave.

"Hold on a minute, now, that you have answered my question, I would like to join you in one of your runs if that is okay with you. It will probably do me some good to go for a healthy run, to take a break from all this moving activity." Mark commented.

Chris hesitated for a moment and pointed out that several groups within the apartment complex meet regularly for a jog or a run. By pointing out the other group of runners, Mark sensed that perhaps, she prefers to run alone. Other than thanking her for the information, he did not pursue the matter any further. She noticed a look of rejection on Mark's face, so she thought of having to clarify her statement.

"Mark, I hope you did not think I was trying to brush you off about going for a run. I just thought of mentioning the various groups of runners that are more consistent and meet regularly. I am more a recreational runner, hardly a disciplined runner. Certainly, you may join me during one of my runs. I would like that." Chris explained

"Chris, there is no need to explain. I fully understand how women should be more cautious with strangers." Mark was trying to lighten up the conversation in hopes to see a smile from Chris.

After she made the statement, she wanted to take it back. If only he knew how complicated her life has been since her four-year relationship ended leaving her with virtually no self-esteem, incapable of interacting with others especially men. Her once friendly, confident, good-natured personality has been over-ridden by distrust, doubtful, disbelief, and seems to be floundering. Being in this mindset, she thought she had enough sense to believe it is not fair for Mark to see her 'dark-side' in full display having just met him recently. She also knows that she does not have the courage or prepared to tell anyone her story.

"Mark, how would you like to change the subject?" Chris asked

"Sure, did you have something in mind?" Mark inquired

"By the way, did you receive the flier on the "Meet-N-Greet" event?" Chris asked

"Yes, I think so, but I did not know what it was about," Mark replied

"The "Meet-N-Greet" event is an invitation to all tenants, both newly moved in tenants, meeting other tenants that have lived here for a while. The apartment management usually provides drinks and appetizers; sometimes a local DJ would provide dance music. It should be fun for someone like you who is new to the State of Washington and meet some of the local people that may have the same hobbies or interest as you do." Chris explained

"Oh, I see. Will you be attending?" Mark quickly asked

"I did not plan on attending this time. I have lived here nearly two years and attended several of these events in the past. My closest friends I met here continue to be my loyal friends. Often, we would get-together for holidays and special occasions. I hope you will get a chance to meet some of the nicest people you will ever meet if you attend the event." Chris added

"I must admit, I am a bit of a loner, not much into the social scene. I prefer a smaller setting. Given a choice, I would rather share a cup of coffee or short visits with friends and neighbors similar to what you and I are having right now." Mark blushed when he realized his statement.

"You have about a month to decide about the event. I hope you change your mind. There will be many people to meet. Here is your opportunity to meet people that have lived here in this state." Chris was trying to convince Mark.

"Likewise, if you change your mind and want to go, I will go too. At least, I will see a familiar face in the crowd. Mark added

"Let me think about it. I will let you know. I had better go. Have a nice evening.

"Good night, Chris," he said

The following afternoon both Chris and Mark happened to arrive at the apartment parking garage at about the same time. Mark saw Chris carrying a couple of bags of groceries just several steps ahead of him. He ran up to her to help her with her bags.

"Hey neighbor looks like you might need a hand with your bags. May I help you with your bags?" Mark asked

Chris hesitated for a moment before she handed him one of the bags. When they reached the foot of the stairs, she turned to him to retrieve her bag. Mark told her he would help carry the bags to her apartment. When they reached her front door, Mark stood by the door, waited for Chris to turn around to collect her bag. Surprisingly, she invited him in as he followed her to her kitchen. Chris directed him to put the bag on the kitchen counter. Mark started to walk towards the front door.

"Thank you, Mark," Chris said

"You are welcome, anytime," he responded

"Mark, can I offer you coffee or tea for your trouble?" Chris asked with a slight nervousness in her voice.

"It is no trouble. That is what neighbors are for, to help each other. I would love a cup of coffee, if you were having a cup." he said

"Have a seat at the counter. How do you take your coffee?" she asked

"I will have black coffee, please," Mark replied

It has been a while since she had a male visitor in her apartment. She was a bit nervous having Mark across the counter from her. Mark sensed her uneasiness while having their coffee. What could have happened to Chris to be somewhat tensed and seemingly uneasy? He started to make small conversation, hoping to put her at ease.

"Chris, have you live here in Washington State all your young life?" he asked

"Yes, I was born in Everett twenty eight years ago. I thought I would add my age in case you were curious. You have this gift of phrasing your questions in a very subtle way that I find very interesting." Chris commented

"You are very perceptive and brilliant. Honestly, I was not fishing for any personal information. Well, perhaps since we are neighbors I am not going to lie and tell you that I would like to get to know you more." Mark stated his honest intentions

Mark noticed that Chris remained quiet for a moment and watched the frown on her face disappearing little by little. Not wanting to overstay his welcome, he decided to finish his coffee and started to get up. Chris must have realized that her silence might be construed as being disinterested in the conversation. On the contrary, she wanted to get to know her new neighbor who has been a gentlemen and respectful. Still, she could not find the courage to let her guards down.

"Mark, I am sorry if I offended you. Just the other day you said I bring out the bad manners in you. I do not think you have any bad manners at all. I seemed to have earned that distinction of being an unfriendly neighbor." Chris looked away as she responded.

"Do not be so hard on yourself. There is nothing wrong with being cautious with strangers. Do you want to know what I think? I think there is a sweet person somewhere in there just wanting to come out. On that note, I should get going." Mark commented

What sweet things to say to someone you have only known for a short time, Chris thought. The kind words coming from Mark gives her encouragement despite the cold fish attitude displayed by Chris. If the situation were different, he just might be the right person that can get her through this awkward time in her life. Nothing could be more real than when she hears the quiet whispers coming from within telling her it is time to move on and begin to face her challenges one at a time. Still, she is unable to take that chance.

"Chris, you seem to be a million miles away. Are you okay?" Mark asked

Mark started to walk around the kitchen counter towards Chris. She got up from the stool where she was sitting to walk Mark to the door. In her mind, she thought Mark could not wait to get the heck out of there. She probably would never see him again. When Mark reached the doorway, he turned around to say good night.

"Chris, I just want to say thank you for the cup of coffee. I hope we can do this again soon. Have a good evening." Mark thought about inviting her out to dinner but held back not wanting to scare her off. As they walked towards the front door, Chris thought of sharing a meal with Mark, but quickly decided against it. Mark extends his hand and just smiled at her as he said good night, then, walked away. Chris gave him a half of smile before saying good night.

It has been about a month since Mark moved into the apartment. The twilight hours last until around 10:00 PM during the summer months. One evening around 9:30 PM, Mark happened to be coming back from emptying his trash when he saw Chris walking up with a trash bag on her way to the trash bins. He waited for her to help her with her bag and wanted to make sure he walks her back to their apartment.

"We have to stop meeting this way. I can think of a thousand places to meet more pleasant than here near the trash bins. Don't you think so?" Mark laughingly commented

Chris could not hold back her spontaneous smile when she heard Mark's comment. She tried to look away to avoid any eye contact with Mark to retreat behind the safety wall she has built for herself to protect her fragile heart.

"Mark, I know you are trying to get me out of my shell. You have the knack to put people at ease and put a smile on their faces. That is refreshing." Chris commented

"I take that as a compliment coming from you. I am glad I ran into you. I wanted to let you know that I will be away on a 3-day trip starting tomorrow morning and I should be back on Sunday night. That must be music to your ear." Mar stated

"Oh, are you going on a mini-vacation?" Chris asked. She thought he is probably going to visit a girlfriend or a wife.

"No, it is strictly a business trip," Mark answered.

"Thank you for informing me. Have a safe trip." Chris said

"Well, you deserve a break from me." Mark smiled as they both walked back to their apartment.

Mark had an early flight Thursday morning. Chris was awakened around 4:00 AM when she heard his door closed. She lay in her bed for a while thinking what a kind and thoughtful person Mark has been, the kind of guy-friend she would like to have. Her instincts about male friends have put on hold since her break-up, but with Mark, it is different. Chris' alarm clock went off which startled her back from her deep thoughts. She, too, needed to get ready for work.

After several days of not seeing Mark or running into him around the apartment complex, Chris caught herself double checking Mark's parking stall to see if he may have come home early. Mark went on his business trip on Thursday and returned late evening Sunday night. On his way to his apartment, he looked up at Chris' unit and saw that her living room lights were still on. He quickly glanced at his watch and saw the time 9:20 PM, probably too late to visit a friend. He decided not to come up to see Chris. As he closed his door, he heard footsteps from upstairs, so he knew Chris was still up. He hesitated for a moment, but something compelled him to come up to at least tell her that he was back.

Chris would usually have a cup of English Earl Tea before going to bed. She thought she heard a light knock at the door just as she placed the tea kettle on the stove. Not expecting anyone that late, she continued to make herself a cup of tea. Then, she heard the light knock again. Chris quietly walked up to look through the peephole to see who would be visiting this late? If only Mark could see the smile on her face the moment she saw Mark on the other side of the door, he would have known he did the right thing by coming up to see her. She quickly opened the door, delighted to see him standing there with a slight smile, but somewhat embarrassed knowing that it was late. Nonetheless, Chris asked him to come in.

"Hey, stranger, did you just get back from your business trip?" Chris greeted Mark with excitement that she almost hugged him, but caught herself.

"I know it is late, but I just wanted to let you know that I am back." He said with some excitement in his voice.

"I was just about to have a cup of tea. Would you like a cup?" she asked.

"That sounds like a good idea," Mark responded as he followed her to the kitchen.

"Have a seat at the counter. How do you take your tea, sugar, honey, lemon or just plain? Have you had dinner?" Chris asked

"Yes, I had dinner at the airport while waiting for my flight, just honey with my tea, please," Mark replied

"Okay, one tea with honey coming up. How was your trip?" Chris asked as she handed him his tea and she sat across the counter from him. Happy to see him back, she wanted to hear about his trip.

"Eeemmm, the tea hit the spot. Thank you." Mark said with much appreciation.

Chris sensed that Mark must be tired from his trip or merely avoiding answering her question. He continued to enjoy his cup of tea. She remembered Mark telling her he came to the State of Washington straight from Europe. Naturally, her curiosity prompted her to ask what brought him to a sleepy town of Everett. Was he just passing through? Mark senses a sincere interest in her question, so he explained his connection with the U.S. Government. Not being too specific about his line of work, he described his job as an independent contractor working with various branches of the U.S. Military Services. The State of Washington plays a vital role in the West Coast strategic military defense both foreign and domestic. Therefore, most of the military personnel become independent contractors when they retire from their military obligations. Chris listened intently as Mark explained his line of work. However, it was getting late, and the next day happened to be a workday for both of them. The tone of his voice indicated a sense of mystery that she wanted to hear more. Perhaps, he has had a long day of traveling and maybe a bit tired from his trip. She decided not to pursue her curiosity any further.

"Well, I didn't mean to bore you with the details about my job. What do you say we save the rest of my story for another day? I just stopped in to let you know I am back." Mark politely stated the purpose of his visit.

"You are right. It is late, and you have had a long day. I am glad you are back. Now, I can sleep much better knowing you are here." Chris admitted.

"Thank you, for the cup of tea and the visit. Good night, Chris." Mark started towards the door, and she was right behind him. Before he opened the door, he turned around and wanted to hug Chris, but changed his mind and just smiled. Chris happened to be looking down and missed the charming look from Mark. Still, Chris sees Mark as a neighbor and determined to remain safe behind the walls she built to protect her fragile being.

CHAPTER 2

FIRST DATE

During the summer months in the state of Washington, you cannot miss the spectacular display of hues in the sky ranging from orange to subtle blue colors in the early evenings. Occasionally, there would be unexpected showers at any time. Chris decided to go for a run, to clear her head regarding a job offer that her boss discussed with her earlier that day. As she walked outside her door, she saw Mark at the foot of the stairs, dressed in shorts, t-shirt, running shoes and a light jacket tied around his waist, doing some stretches, seemingly waiting for her to go on a run. Seeing Mark put a smile on her face.

"Hey, there, may I tag along on your run?" Mark politely asked. He suggested stopping in at the coffee shop on the way back.

"That sounds like a good idea. Yes, we can stop at Starbucks just around the corner." Chris agreed. She remained quiet during the initial run. Mark noticed the concerned look on her face.

"Are you okay? You have not said much since we started the run." Mark asked

"It is nothing that a good cup of coffee could not fix." Chris quickly answered

"You sound as though you have a lot on your mind. Would you rather go for a cup of coffee now? Mark asked

"I need some advice on work-related matters. It can wait until after we go for a short run." Chris sounded as if she needed a friend for advice.

They took the short route around the neighborhood and towards a famous beach where most runners/joggers prefer to run because of the wide path, and there are no cars allowed in the area.

Chris started to open up the conversation. "I work for World-Wide Aeronautics Company here in Everett in the Human Resources Department. The company needed to expand and decided to build a second location in Raleigh, South Carolina, which happens to be a state with "Right-To-Work" law, differs from a union shop here in Everett. Not to worry, I will not bore you with the details. Because of a different set of laws, rules, and regulations, a new HR department must be created prior to completion of the new location in South Carolina. Since my background and workexperience has been in business law, my boss asked me to consider applying for the new position that will be posted next week. Two potential candidates are being recommended for the position, but he asked if he could submit my name. I felt honored and humbled to be considered for the job, but I am not sure it is the right job for me at this time. The new location might be interesting for someone to start a new life." Chris made a revealing statement that caught Mark by surprise.

"It sounds like a critical job with a lot of responsibilities. Is it something you would like to do in the future?" Mark asked

"It is a dream job that I hope to have someday. I am only twenty-eight years old, probably not mature enough to take on such a demanding job. One of my biggest concerns would be my confidence to do the job." Chris declared.

Mark wisely noted, "Age is just a number and not a factor in job qualifications. Your boss picked you because he is confident you can do the job unless he has other motives. May I ask a very personal question? You do not have to answer. Is there a romantic interest in this job offer?" Mark reluctantly asked.

Chris quickly responded, "No, not at all, he is happily married to Heidi, and they have two boys starting college in the fall. Speaking of college, just before I graduated from college I applied at World-Wide Aeronautics for internship. I was accepted then, hired me as a full-time employee. My boss has been a mentor and like a father-figure to me, I seek his advice after my difficult breakup, which may have prompted the South Carolina offer. That is another story for another time."

"Chris, I am going to be direct with you, please just tell me when to stop talking. I sensed several things going on with you that may be affecting your decision. You mentioned a recent breakup that you cannot talk about, and you have this job offer, do you think your overall confidence about your work may have been taken aback by your recent breakup?" he asked, then, he added, "You will need to differentiate between the two situations. Otherwise, you will second guess yourself and doubt your capabilities and confidence should you face a similar situation in the future."

Chris stopped running for a moment and turned to Mark to say, "How did you get so smart about life? You are reading me so well it is scary. What else do you see or want to know?"

Just at that moment, big raindrops started coming down. It was a clear night when they began their run. Now, the big drops turned into rain. They both started running faster, but they were about a mile away from their apartment complex. Mark saw a bus stop with small roofing that may shelter them from the rain temporarily. He grabbed Chris by the hand to the bus stop and took off his jacket to put it around her. She was shaking from the cold rain that came suddenly. Mark held her close to him to share his body heat.

"I am so cold." her voice was shaking, "Thank you for the jacket. What about you, are you okay?" Chris asked

He responded, "I am fine, how about you? It is raining even harder. I could run home, get the car and get you. Will you be all right by yourself?"

"I would rather run home with you then stay here. Let us wait for a few more minutes and see if the rain lets up." She suggested

They sat on the bench, Mark holding Chris close to him as she sat quietly on his lap. The rain started to ease up a little. They decided to make a run for it and finally reached the apartment complex, both completely drenched.

"I am so glad you were with me," Chris told Mark. "I think I am going upstairs to get out of these wet clothes and take a hot bath. You probably should do the same thing before you catch a cold." She added, "May I take your jacket and wash it with these clothes?"

"A hot bath sounds like a good idea. You do not need to wash my jacket. I can just add it to the rest of my clothes. I will take it.," he said

Chris started to remove the jacket and handed it to Mark. "Thank you for the jacket. "Good night, Mark."

"Good night, Chris. Sorry, we did not get a chance to have that cup of coffee." Mark waited until Chris entered her apartment and heard the door closed before he went inside.

The following morning they ran into each other in the parking garage. Mark was just about to get in his car when he saw Chris just walking towards her parking stall. He walked towards her to say hello.

"Hi, neighbor, good to see you this morning. That was quite a rain storm we had last night. Is that normal this time of the year?" Mark commented.

"Hi, Mark, how are you? It was unexpected because there were so many stars in the sky last night. Thank you for sharing your jacket with me and keeping me company. You just witnessed how a perfect night can quickly change into something else without any warning." Chris explained

"I see what you mean. How would you like to continue our conversation about your job offer over a cup of coffee or dinner?" Mark asked.

"You and I must be on the same wavelength because I was going to ask you if you would like to share a casserole tonight or tomorrow night," Chris stated

"That is a better offer than mine. I would love to share that homemade casserole with you. If it is not too short of notice, I am available for dinner tonight." Mark was anxious to have that homemade dinner prepared by Chris and the pleasure of her company." Mark looked excited about the invitation.

"Perfect, I took a half a day off for my dentist appointment in the afternoon. I should be home early to get dinner started. How is six-thirty PM for dinner at my apartment sound to you?" Chris suggested

"Can I bring a bottle of wine or something? I am not much on dessert except a bowl of ice cream." Mark stated.

"That is a wonderful idea to bring the wine. It does not matter red or white. I will see you later around six-thirty." Chris added.

"Yup, have a good day." Mark walked away with a smile on his face.

The anticipation of having dinner with Chris, Mark found himself whistling and smiling all day long, which he has not done in a long time. On his way home, he stopped at the flower shop to pick up some flowers. As soon as he got back, he took a shower and put on a nice shirt and jeans. He kept looking at his watch, acting like a teenager going on his first date. It was precisely six-thirty when he walked up the stairs and knocked on her door.

Equally excited about the dinner date with Mark, she changed her wardrobe at least three times. She barely got her shoes on when she heard the knock at the door.

"Hello neighbor, just in time. Come in." Chris immediately saw the beautiful bouquet of flowers and the bottle of wine that Mark brought.

Wow! Chris looked stunning in her yellow summer dress, with her hair down to her shoulders. He could not stop looking at her. In his mind, he debated whether to compliment her or just leave it alone. He handed her the flowers.

"These are for you and this bottle of wine is for us. It smells good in here," he said

"Mark, the flowers are beautiful, perfect for the table, thank you. Can I get you anything to drink other than a glass of wine? I have some sparkling water and soda. What would you like?" Chris asked

"Just a glass of wine would be just fine. Would you like me to open the bottle?" Mark asked

"Yes, please. The glasses are on the table. Go ahead and pour me a glass of wine too while I take out the casserole. Take either seat you like." she said

The table setting looked so lovely and arranged beautifully. The colorful flowers brought out the subtle colors on the tablecloth, accentuated by the red cloth napkins. The white plates and crystal stemware completed the table setting. It has a woman's touch all over it. The aroma of freshly baked casserole right out of the oven activated the sense of smell which sends a strong message that – it is time to eat.

"Before we start dinner, I would like to welcome you to Everett,

Washington officially. I hope you will like it here and stay a while. Cheers!" Chris welcomed Mark to the neighborhood

"Thank you for the warm welcome. Having neighbors like you, I am sure I will be here for a long time." Mark responded

"Let's toast to our long friendship and hopefully, you will like the casserole," Chris added as they both laugh.

"Eeemmm, this is delicious. Is this recipe something you can share?" Mark commented.

"Are you just flattering the cook or are you serious about wanting the recipe?" she responded

"Well, if I wanted to compliment the chef, I would say, you look simply stunning in your yellow dress." He blushed when he complimented her.

"I know you are just being your kind self and have lots of compliments to dish out. Nevertheless, I appreciate the compliments, and yes, I will give you the recipe." Chris responded.

"I do mean what I said about how nice you look in your dress. You reminded me of frosty lemonade on a hot day, cool, light and refreshing." Mark being charming but he meant it.

"Oh, by the way, I need to warn you about my low tolerance for alcohol. So, if I get silly, you have my permission to slap me back to my senses." Chris mentioned.

"Thank you for the warning, but I would neither "slap" a woman nor lay a hand on lady regardless of how silly they may get," Mark said it with a stern seriousness. He went on to say, "Just exactly how silly do you get, just joking?"

Chris surprisingly replied with a smile on her face, "I tend to be giddy, happy, somewhat daring and if I am with a man I like I am more relax and affectionate. Do not worry; having known you only a short time you are safe at this time. Shall we change the subject? Have you decided if you were going to attend the "Meet-N-Greet" event?" Chris asked

"Oh, I have completely forgotten about the event. Is that happening this Friday?" Mark inquired

"Yes, it is this Friday. It has been a while since I have gone to one

of these, so I told my friends I would help them set up the food table."
Chris responded

"Do you need some help with setting up? I have these strong biceps
that can be put to use if needed." Mark showed his muscles for grins.

"I am sure we can use some help in the clubhouse. Did you have
enough to eat? I know you said you are not into dessert, but would you
like a bowl of ice cream? We can have our coffee or tea in the living
room where it is more comfortable." Chris stated

Good memory! Yes, I would love a bowl of ice cream. Can I help
you with the dishes?" Mark commented.

"Let me get the bowls and let you dish out the ice cream for both of
us while I clear the table. I will take two scoops of ice cream, please."
Chris requested

They agreed on delegation of responsibilities almost sounding like
an old married couple. The effect of having some wine during dinner
seemed to have created a more relax and mellow atmosphere for Mark
and Chris. While they had their bowl of ice cream in the living room,
they kept their conversation short and talked in general. Mark asked
questions about the state of Washington such as seasonal weather, sports
fishing, and hunting, recommended tourist sites, favorite eating places,
etc. As the evening continued, their conversation became somewhat
probing and inquisitive, wanting to find out more about the other
person. Chris wanted to know about Mark's travels, how it ties in with
his job, and what brought him to a small town like Everett. Surprisingly,
Mark seems receptive to Chris's curiosity.

"Thanks again for the delicious dinner, great dessert, terrific
conversation, and a gracious host. Next time, it will be my turn to cook
dinner for you. Having spent some time in Italy, I can make some Italian
cuisine that might surprise you. Instead of talking about my culinary
talents, I hope to have the opportunity to put my reputation on the
line by cooking for you. Now, let us resume our discussion on your job
offer." Mark remembered that she needed some advice on work-related
matters.

"Mark, I must admit having had a full glass of wine my mind is not
focused on the job offer. I do not have the clarity I need to carry on a
conversation on the subject intelligently. If it is okay with you, I would

like to hear more about you and how you happened to move to a little town like Everett, Washington, which is almost on the opposite side of the world?" Chris implored.

"Well, let me start by saying I am thirty-one years old, single, never been married. I spent my younger years back East where most of my family still reside. After high school, I applied and accepted at the Annapolis Military College where I graduated and joined the U.S. Navy to become a helicopter pilot. When I got out of my military obligation, I became an independent defense contractor for the U.S. Government. My work assignments have taken me to Europe, Asia, Africa, USA and the Middle East. Coming to the West Coast is a first for me." Mark paused for a moment to look at Chris just to see if she had any questions or comments. She seemed to be listening intently and had the look of wanting to hear more.

Chris commented, "Since you are on a roll, please continue with your story. We can talk about my job offer another day. I want to hear more about your travels, what exactly you do that takes you to so many interesting places that most people can only dream about, so please continue." Chris sounded more interested in Mark's story.

"As you may have noticed, my job is not your typical nine to five job. When "Uncle Sam" calls on you, you say, when and where. There are times when my job requires me to be away on business trips, not knowing how long I would be gone. Fortunately, I love to travel and have the flexibility of being able to be on the go for my next assignment. I am pretty much a loner, which works well for me. " Mark admitted.

"You don't talk much about your trips or travels, which I find intriguing and mysterious. Is your line of work something I would read about in a mystery spy novel, like a covert agent or some sort of a spy on assignment or a secret mission?" Chris asked with a sense of playfulness, yet, with a great deal of curiosity.

Still, acting playful, Chris watched Mark's reaction. She noticed the change of look on his face as if she struck a nerve. Mark's face became serious for a moment and had the look of something that caught him by surprise.

"What makes you think I am some sort of a spy or a secret agent?" Mark asked half kiddingly and somewhat a serious question.

"This is the silliness I was talking about earlier. See, what I told you about my low tolerance for alcohol. I get silly and loopy, out in "la-la land" so to speak. I have been reading too many spy novels that my imaginations tend to run away from me especially after a glass of wine. I am sorry if I went overboard by asking too many questions about what you do. Before I make a fool of myself on full display, we probably should call it a night. It has been a fun night." Chris said it endearingly.

"I have had a wonderful time. I think you ask brilliant questions. You have been a most gracious hostess, and your hospitality is beyond description. I am fortunate to have you as my neighbor. Next time, we will talk about your job offer." Mark sincerely enjoyed their time together.

"Thank you, kind sir. I have had a lovely time. I am sure we will have more times like this. What are you doing tomorrow night, just kidding?" Chris was smiling.

They both walked towards the door. Mark had been thinking about how he should say good night, with or without a hug. As they reached the door, Chris gave Mark a hug and a kiss on the cheek. He wanted to kiss her back to the lips but hesitated not wanting to be inappropriate for their first dinner date together.

"Good night, Chris, thank you for a delightful evening," Mark said
"You are welcome, Mark, good night," Chris responded.

Chris had a smile on her face as she closed the door. If Mark had kissed her on the lips, she would not have resisted. However, she knows that wanting affection from Mark would not be real. One thing for sure, their compatibility felt natural and effortless.

Mark was unable to fall asleep right away. He reflected back on his dinner date with Chris. He had a good time and saw her as someone he would like to get to know more. Not only is she a good looking gal, but she also possesses natural qualities such as sweetness, sincerity, kindness, and playfulness that are charming and appealing, yet, there is a sense of sadness and restlessness behind her demeanor. She has a big decision to make regarding her job situation and her recent breakup. Mark intends to be a good friend to Chris and support her during her time of need.

CHAPTER 3

MEET-AND-GREET EVENT

Thursday evening, Chris went on her run at the usual time six PM. Mark must not be home yet because there were no lights in his apartment. By the time she got back from her run still, no lights. Chris proceeded to her apartment and took a shower. She started to fix herself a sandwich when she heard a knock at the door. She looked through the peephole and saw Mark standing there.

"Hey, there, did you just get home? Have you had dinner?" Chris asked.

"I was at Lacey Air Force Base today to meet up with other teammates in the area. Coming back to Everett, I ran into heavy traffic just past Seattle due to a partial closure of a bridge. It took me four and a half hours just to get back to Everett. Anyway, I just stopped by to ask what time did you want to head out to the clubhouse tomorrow?" Mark stated. He added, "Yes, I would love a sandwich if it is not too much trouble. Is it that obvious that I look hungry?" Mark said with a smile

"You are in luck. I happen to have some extra meatloaf. How would you like a meatloaf sandwich? What would you like to drink with your sandwich?" Chris asked

"If you have any wine left from last night, I will have a glass. If it is okay with you, I can help myself with the drinks. What would you like to drink?" Mark asked

"I will have a glass of sparkling water, please. Go ahead and help yourself with the wine and have a seat at the counter. I will bring the sandwiches." Chris said

Chris watched Mark eat his sandwich as she sat across the counter from him, making small conversation allowing him to eat his meal. Although they have only known each other for a short time, she felt safe and comfortable having Mark around her that she had not felt in a long time.

"The sandwich sure hit the spot, thank you. What time did you want me to pick you up tomorrow night?" Mark asked

"You are welcome. I told Sandy and Lorraine that I would help them set up the refreshment and food table. I am meeting them as soon as I get home. You can meet me there." Chris stated

"What time is the event supposed to start?" Mark asked

"The party starts at seven PM. There will be appetizers and various drinks at the event," Chris added

"Do you ladies need some help setting up for the event? I have an early start tomorrow morning and should be home early if you need assistance tomorrow? Just come by the apartment. I should go, unless you want me to stay to talk about your job offer." Mark stated.

"Thank you for the offer, but I have a few more days before I have to decide to apply for the job or not`. Go on and scoot along. I will see you tomorrow." Chris gave Mark a quick hug at the door.

The day of the meet-and-greet event finally arrived. Mark was waiting for Chris to get home to walk over to the clubhouse. He gave her a few minutes before he went upstairs. Chris was just walking out of her apartment when he stepped outside his apartment.

"That was perfect timing. Did you have a good day?" Chris asked.

"Yes, I had a good day. I am looking forward to this event and meeting your friends." Mark commented.

When they got to the clubhouse, Chris saw all her friends there – Tom, Marie, Sandy, and Lorraine. Tom had his cowboy hat on his head and wearing his usual western attire while the women wore a casual party dress. Both Chris and Mark walked over to her friends to make the introduction.

"Hello everyone, I would like you all to meet my new neighbor, Mark Ingram. He is new to the state of Washington. "Chris introduced

Mark. Each one of her friends took turns introducing them to Mark, starting with Tom.

"Hello, Mark, I am Tom McKenzie, and this is my wife Marie, the love of my life for almost twenty-five blissful years." Tom turned to Marie with an endearing look as he introduced his wife. He gave Mark a firm handshake with both hands. Marie followed her husband by extending her hand to shake Mark's hand. Lorraine was somewhat shy, so she also smiled at Mark and shook his hand.

"Finally, last but not least I am Sandy Clark, one of the co-hosts of the event with my partner in crime, Lorraine. It has been a while since Chris attended one of these events. What did you have to do to get her in here?" Sandy commented.

Sandy's outgoing personality fits her nickname as "Ms. Social Butterfly" of the group. Right away, she took Mark by the hand, so that she can introduce him to other neighbors. Smitten by Mark's good looks and the charisma he emits naturally, it did not take her long before Sandy started flirting with Mark. She continued to dominate Mark's attention by taking him away from Chris' circle of friends. In the meantime, Chris pretty much stayed with her close friends but kept one eye on Mark. Out of nowhere, a new face who claims to be a new neighbor of Tom and Marie came by and introduced himself as one of Tom's new friends that recently moved into the apartment complex.

"Hello, my name is Larry Edison, possibly a distant relative to Thomas Edison, the inventor. I am Tom and Marie's new neighbor. Who do I have the pleasure of their company?" Larry must have used that same pickup line to charm Chris and Loraine.

"My name is Lorraine Simms, one of the co-hosts of the event. This is Chris Jensen who lives in the same building as I do." Lorraine made the introduction

Right away, Larry turned on his debonair charm and held his hand out to shake their hand. Mimicking a continental gentleman, he reached for their hand and added a kiss. The girls just looked at each other somewhat annoyed. He tried to impress the ladies by describing some of the yacht parties he has recently attended. The more he talked, the less impressed the ladies became. He sounded like a used car salesman desperately selling fake goods.

"I see you beautiful ladies do not have a drink. What can I get you to drink?" Larry insisted.

"We would like some ginger ale, please." Chris quickly responded just to get a break from all of Larry's fake charm. She turned to Lorraine, and they both had a smirk look on their face as if to say, "enough already."

"I think he likes you," Lorraine commented

"He's cute, but not my type. He needs to tone down that annoying charm of his. I am sure he will find someone here before the night is over, not me." Chris said firmly without any hesitation.

Larry came back with several drinks for the girls. Both Chris and Lorraine asked for ginger ale. Instead, he brought them other alcoholic mixed drinks and handed them to the ladies. Chris reluctantly accepted the drink knowing her tolerance for alcohol. Larry turned up his charm in an attempt to get Chris' attention. He continued to carry on a conversation with both ladies while Chris kept one eye on Mark and Sandy. Larry excused himself to get another refill on his drink. Chris immediately placed her glass on another table before Larry came back. Both girls commented how they needed a break from Larry. Lorraine added she hoped he would get lost and not come back. Chris could not agree more with Lorraine's comment as they both chuckled.

"Oh, my, he is quite a flirt. You know he is smitten by your smile because he raised his charm to even higher level. It would not surprise me if he went home with someone." Lorraine commented

"That must be his mission. I am sure he will find someone before the night is over." Chris commented

The DJ started playing lovely music, and people began to dance. Chris saw Larry approaching their way, probably to ask for a dance. He came to ask Chris if she would like to dance. Not wanting to be rude to Tom and Marie's neighbor, she obliged with some hesitation.

"Would you like to test the dance floor?" Larry asked

"I am not a very good dancer. You might want to reconsider your options." Chris quickly responded

"Neither am I, not a very good dancer. I will try not to step on your toes." Larry said

"Okay, let me just put my drink down." Chris started to walk to the table.

"Where is your drink? Let me get you another one, be right back." Larry insisted.

When Larry came back with a couple of drinks, Chris began making small talk. "Are you new to Everett, Washington? How do you like living here? My goodness, this drink is very strong. I have a low tolerance when it comes to heavy liquor. You should have gotten me some ginger ale." Chris protested.

Larry pretended that he did not hear Chris' comment. They continued to dance. After a while, the crowd grew to near full capacity. Sandy kept Mark by her side, occasionally introducing him to other tenants. Mark focused on just watching Chris with Larry, who took the liberty of dominating Chris's company. Mark noticed that Chris and Larry were getting cozy on the dance floor. Larry's hands were all over Chris while dancing. She has a low tolerance for alcohol that seemed to have distorted her senses. Mark asked Sandy to dance so he can get a closer look at Chris and Larry. Something did not look right when Mark got closer and saw Chris's eyes looked glossy, seemingly not aware of her surroundings. Sandy tried to flirt with Mark by asking provocative questions.

"So, Mark, I hear you are new to the area. Did you just go through a breakup or something else? A good-looking guy like you cannot be single for long. Can I take you home tonight?" Sandy propositioned Mark playfully but awaiting an answer.

"I am flattered, but I know you are kidding. No, I did not break up with anyone. I have been out of the country for five years. My job took me here to Everett, Washington. I like this state. There are many outdoor activities to do here. How long have you lived here?" Mark politely responded to Sandy. He continued to keep an eye on Chris as he grew more concern by the way she seemed to just hang on to Larry.

"I have lived in Washington State all my life, born and raised in Seattle until I moved to Everett five years ago." Sandy was a flirt.

Mark could not stand it any longer, watching Larry manhandle Chris that way. There must be something wrong because Chris hardly moved. When the song ended, and another song started, Mark took Sandy back to where Lorraine, Tom, and Marie were just chatting. He excused himself and said he would be back. Mark walked over to where Larry and Chris were dancing.

"Excuse me, but may I cut in to speak with my neighbor for a few minutes, please? I have not said hello to her. Would you mind if I danced with her?" Mark politely asked

"I will let you cut in for one dance. I am going to get a drink, then, I want her back." Larry reluctantly handed Chris over to Mark, a bit perturbed that Mark interrupted their dance.

"Hey, Chris, are you enjoying the party?" Mark asked. Chris was not responding. She just seems to be just hanging on to Mark like a rag doll. He asked again, "Chris, are you all right?" He waited for a couple of seconds, looking at her glazed eyes. She just seemed to be sleepy.

"Mark, can you please take me home. I am not feeling so well. My head is spinning, and I can hardly feel my legs underneath me." Chris complained.

"Sure, where is your sweater? Oh, I see it. Sit here, and I will get your stuff. I will be right back. Let us get out of here. " Mark and Chris exited to a side door and got out before Larry came back.

Chris could hardly walk without some assistance from Mark. She almost fell, but Mark caught her and scooped her up to carry her to her apartment. She was having difficulty finding her keys until Mark helped her. He sat her down on the couch and started to gag as if she wanted to throw up. Mark walked her to the bathroom where she threw up in the toilet; her body seems to be convulsing at the same time. This does not look normal from alcohol drinking. A few minutes later, he helped her back into the living room and sat her on the couch. Not long after he sat her down, there was a knock at the door. It was Larry, drunk as a skunk. He opened the door with the look of disdain towards Larry.

"Hey, man, what did you do with my girl?" Larry reeked of alcohol.

"I want to know what you put in her drink, you son-of-a-bitch," Mark said in an outraged tone.

"I did not put anything in her drink. I want to see her." Larry demanded.

"Get the hell out of here before I call the cops. I am going to count to three; you better be out of sight." Mark meant what he said. He had a phone in his hand and was getting ready to call the cops.

Larry staggered down the stairway, almost falling from being drunk. He did not put up much of a fight, not wanting to see any cops. Mark was just about to call the police when Chris was trying to stand up looking scared. Mark went to her right away.

"What kind of drinks did that son-of-a-bitch Larry gave you? Did he give you any pills to take? Do you remember what you were drinking?" Mark asked the questions, so in case he has to take her to the hospital he would be prepared.

"I do not know. The last drink tasted kind of spicy and burning sensation. I did not see any pills, why?" Chris was slowly coming around, and after she threw up some of the alcohol in her stomach, she felt better.

"That a-hole must have given you something like a "date rape drugs" in your drink. Cowards like him would give the girls drugs when they cannot get their way. I want to go over there and turn him into the police. Stay away from him. How are you feeling? Do you want to go to ER?" he asked

"I think I will be all right. I feel so much better now that I throw up. My head is still spinning, and my legs feel weak." Chris described how she felt. Still, shivering while sitting on the couch, she asked Mark to help her to her bedroom, so that she could get under the covers and warm up. He removed her shoes, fully clothed in her party dress, she shook more strongly, so Mark looked around her bedroom for another blanket, but was unable to find any. He still had his jacket and shoes on, so he decided to wrap her up on top of the cover, put his arm around her to share his body heat. Her body started to respond and not shake so vigorously. He rocked her like a baby. She began to move her arms around his neck and started to kiss his chin, face, then his lips. She continued to kiss him passionately and positioned herself on top of him. As a warm-blooded man, he has his wants and desires too, until he realized, that her false passions were a result of the date rape drugs that were still in her system. He put a stop to it right away and got up from the bed. Chris was confused and unaware of what she was doing. She laid there for a moment until she came to her senses. Mark has so much respect for her that he was not going to have her that way. Mark went to the living room and sat quietly in one of the wing chairs. He heard Chris come out from her bedroom. She sat on the couch, feeling somewhat embarrassed by her behavior.

"Mark, I am so sorry for misbehaving, not knowing what came over me. I do not know what prompted me to do that. I am truly sorry. Under different circumstances, as a woman, my ego would have been devastated because you rejected my advances. However, you honored me by respecting me enough to know that it was not right. That, my friend, sets you apart from winners and losers, like Larry. No doubt, you are a man of honor and integrity, a winner." Chris was honoring Mark as a real man.

"I am happy to hear that you understood my actions. I would not have wanted it any other way with you. I hope you know that." Mark hoped that would be her understanding.

"Just curious, what made you come up to me when you did? What was Larry doing to me that set the alarm to check up on me?" Chris inquired

"The moment he laid eyes on you, he meant trouble. He was smooth and slick like a shaving cream that needed "wiping" off immediately. As the night progressed, his hands were all over you. In his sick mind, he was making love to you in front of everyone. What alarmed me was that you were just standing there, not moving very much. When I came up to you, I knew something was wrong. Do you want to press charges? He will likely do it again to another girl. Part of my training was to recognize specific human behavior due to drugs. I saw it playing out in front of me that is why I intervened. Otherwise, he would have gotten his way if no one stopped him. You may feel a little better, but there are residual side effects in your system for about twenty-four to forty-eight hours, depending on the drugs he gave you.

"Maybe, a hot shower and a good night sleep will get rid of these toxins in my system. You should go and get some rest. You saved my life. I do not know how to thank you for what you did." Chris declared.

"You are giving me way too much credit. I saw a damsel in distress that needed rescuing. It was the right thing to do. Unfortunately, Larry will not give up until he gets his way. In case he shows up again, I think I should stay here tonight." Mark suggested

"You will need a pillow and a blanket. I will go get them." Chris did not hesitate to accept Mark's offer to stay.

As Chris was prepping the couch for Mark, she tried to avoid any eye contact, feeling the embarrassment of her earlier behavior. Even though she felt safe having Mark watch over her, she felt awkward having a man just a few feet from her bedroom. Mark sensed her nervousness of being in her apartment.

"Chris, would you like to sit for a couple of minutes, so that I can explain some possible reactions from the drugs in your system. For the next twenty-four hours, you might experience muscle weakness in your legs, a hangover, nausea and feeling anxious or anxiety. Just holler, if you need some help. Taking a hot bath will help with keeping you warm. Get lots of rest and drink plenty of fluids should get rid of some of the foreign residuals in your system. I will be just outside your room. Good night and see you in the morning." Mark explained

"Yes, sir, I am glad you are staying." Chris quietly responded

"Lastly, you did not do anything wrong to fell any embarrassment on your action. The effect of the drugs in your system distorted your behavior. Do not hesitate to call the authorities if he comes near you. On that note, we better get some sleep." Mark said

"Thank you for saying that. Good night, Mark." she sad

"Good night, Chris." he gave her a smile

The following morning, Chris got up to check on Mark. He had already gone. The pillows and blanket were neatly folded and placed on the couch. She turned the coffee pot on and started to make breakfast when the doorbell rang. The first thing that came to her mind, Mark must have come back to check up on her. It brought a slight smile on her face, so she hurriedly ran to the door without looking through the peephole. When she opened the door, she felt the anxiety rushing through her body upon seeing Larry standing just a step away in front of her.

"Good morning, sunshine. May I come in?" Larry was trying to be sweet.

"No, I do not think so. You better leave now." Chris commanded

"I just want to talk to you about last night. May I come in?" Larry pleaded

Mark was just coming up the stairs when he yelled up, "You heard her. She does not want you to come in. You had better leave. Chris, lock the door and call 911." Mark instructed Chris.

"I do not want to start any trouble. I just want to apologize for last night." Larry begged

"Say your apologies and get the hell out of here and stay away from her or you will have to deal with me," Mark spoke in a fiery tone

Larry left abruptly. Mark came upstairs to check on Chris. The moment they made eye contact, Mark saw the fear in her eyes as she stood in the middle of the room seemingly frozen unable to move. Mark walked up to her to put his arms around her. Chris held on to Mark tightly, not wanting to let go. He could feel her body trembling as she cried uncontrollably. They held on to each other for a few minutes as Mark caressed her back to ease some of the tension. Chris was frightened by the whole incident that she would not let go her grip on Mark. He took her into the kitchen to get her something to drink. He thought of giving her a shot of whiskey, but it was too early, and coffee or tea would not be strong enough to calm her down. He went ahead and gave her half a shot of whiskey. Like a real trooper, she took the drink. Her low tolerance to alcohol the half shot immediately gave her a buzz. In a matter of minutes, she slowly relaxed, easing up her grip on Mark. The look of fear suddenly changed to anger. Chris started to pace back and forth seemingly in deep thoughts.

"Are you all right?" Mark asked

She nodded her head, but still, she did not want to say anything. She wanted to get dressed so that she can get a restraining order on Larry to stay as far away from her as possible. She asked Mark if he could take her to the city hall.

"Chris, it is Saturday morning. City Hall and government offices are closed. We can call the authorities and see what we can do." Mark stated

Mark contacted local authorities while Chris sat nearby listening to the conversation. Chris wanted to report the incident to get a restraining order. Without giving full details, there is an outstanding warrant for Larry's arrest filed in the town of Marysville. An officer was dispatched to Chris' residence to get a full incident report on what happened. After the officer completed the report, she was advised that a temporary restraining order is in effect until a formal order is granted from the local courts. Chris would have to go to court on Monday to appear in front of a judge for the restraining order. Mark decided to go with her to provide some support.

"I do not know how to thank you for all the support you have given me. I will be forever grateful for your friendship." Chris sincerely meant every word she said to Mark. They have only known each other for a short time, yet, they have struck a connection to an unforeseen destiny that will tie them forever

A week has passed since the Larry incident. No word from the authorities as to Larry's whereabouts except his apartment has been under surveillance for any activities. The tenants have been given description and pictures of Larry, with a warning to report any knowledge or sighting of the suspect. Finally, a local TV station in Everett reported on an arrest of Larry Edison in Seattle area for an assault on a young woman. The authorities notified Chris to confirm Larry's arrest in Seattle. Due to several severe charges against Larry, he will likely be in prison for a long time. No one could be more relieved about the news than Chris. She went downstairs to tell Mark about the report on Larry, but he was not home. She sat on the stairs for a while enjoying the fresh air. Mark came around the corner and found Chris sitting at the foot of the stairs with a smile on her face.

"Hey, what are you doing out here?" Mark sat beside her

"Larry has been arrested, and he is in jail in Seattle as we speak." Chris blurted out the words, with excitement in her voice.

"When did this happen?" Mark asked

"I just received the call from the authorities notifying me of Larry's arrest." Chris quickly responded

"This calls for a celebration. Would you like…" Mark stopped in mid-sentence

"Would you like to have …" Chris spoke at the same time as Mark

"Ladies first, what were you going to ask?" Mark said.

"I was going to ask if you would like to come up and have a cup of coffee or tea," Chris explained.

"That's funny; I was about to ask you if you would like to walk over to Starbucks and have coffee or tea? Since you beat me to it, my answer is yes." Mark gladly replied.

They both walked up to Chris' apartment. Mark wanted to hear more details on Larry's arrest. Chris walked towards the kitchen as Mark followed behind her.

"Would you like coffee or tea?" Chris asked

"A cup of coffee would be great. Having been in the military, you learn to welcome anything hot or lukewarm, often it is usually cold and sometimes just colored water. The short answer would be – black coffee." Mark explained with a smile

Chris brought two cups and a small tray of creamer, sugar, cinnamon, biscotti, etc. There was a look of puzzlement on Mark's face as Chris brought the coffee pot and placed it on the counter.

"I have not served in the military, so forgive me for having some "guilty pleasures" with my coffee that are on this tray. I promise you will always have hot coffee in my house. May I pour you some coffee, sir?" Chris was teasing Mark to get his reaction. They both burst out laughing at what just happened.

"I get it, no more military comments," Mark admitted.

"Okay, let's change the subject. Now, that Larry is history, we can talk about just about anything. His name will never pass my lips ever again." Chris seemed excited

"Oh, no, with all due respect I am not falling into that trap. When a woman says she is willing to talk about anything, it is an invitation for trouble. I will yield to you on the subject that you want to talk about. So, here is your moment. I am all ears." Mark said with a slight chuckle. Chris joined in on the laughter.

"Oh, Mark, I gave you the opening to ask me any question about me. You blew your opportunity to get to know me. Perhaps, you really do not want to know me, if so, the subject is close." Chris stated to get a reaction from Mark

"You are wrong. On the contrary, I want to know more about you," he said

"Okay, let me start by telling you about my circle of friends, who are like a second family to me. You already know about Lorraine and Sandy.

That leaves only Tom and Marie. They are like my parents. Tom is a principal at a nearby high school. He is getting ready to retire after being in the school education for nearly twenty-five years. Marie just retired as a registered nurse. She does volunteer work at Children's Hospital in Seattle. They are originally from Florida. They are genuine and loyal people who I feel fortunate to have them as good friends. Sandy and Lorraine are like my sisters. Lorraine has a fiancé that is currently serving in the Middle East. I am not sure when he is due to come back. Would you like more coffee?" Chris asked

"Yes, please," he said

After Mark listened intently to Chris talk warm-heartedly about her friends, he sensed that Chris seems to have a lot in her mind. He wants so much to help her open up more and earn her trust.

Ever since Mark told her that her recent breakup maybe clouding her decision about the Director's job. He could not have been more accurate with his assessment because her breakup seemed to have consumed all her confidence, including her ambition to become a Director. Moreover, she has trust issues with men, exercising sound judgment and lacking self-worth.

CHAPTER 4

BROKEN HEART AND SPIRIT

"Chris, I have been meaning to ask you the latest on your job offer. Have you decided what you are going to do about the job?" Mark asked

"I had lunch with my boss today. The Director's job will be officially posted in a couple of days, and the posting will close after a week. Then, the job interview will be scheduled as soon as they select the candidates. Since there are officially two positions open, Everett, Washington and Raleigh, South Carolina, Both jobs will be effective October first. This will allow enough time for the new director to find a place to live, move the family, settle in, orientation, etc. My boss gave me a preview of what is expected from the new Director, long work hours, almost no vacation time for the first six months to meet the grueling expectations and goals to make the transition a success. Despite all the challenges, he believed I have the leadership, working knowledge, and the capabilities to become successful if I want the job.

"Your boss sounds like he has complete confidence in you. He supports you 100% as I do. Chris, do you want the job?" Mark sounded excited when he asked

"Mark, I wish I had that confidence. It is complicated for me at the moment. There is more that you don't know about me, not even my closest friends that I trust wholeheartedly." Right then, tears started to fall on Chris's face as she started to reveal more about herself. She went on to say, "Sometimes I merely exist, no confidence, lacking judgment, no sense of direction and the worst part is being in a vacuum feeling hopelessness and losing my sense of self-worth." Her tears came down profusely as she lowered her head not wanting to face Mark.

Mark quickly came around the counter to Chris's side to hug her tightly, not saying anything and just allowing her to cry on his shoulder. She held on to him seemingly not wanting to let go.

"Let it all out, just hang on to the thought that you have good friends that love you and support you, more importantly, you are not alone. You have good friends that are ready and willing to help you through this ordeal. I am here." Mark simply stated his sincere thoughts. "Chris, I am going to sit you down and want you to listen to me for a few minutes. Would you like some water to drink?" Mark asked.

"Yes, please, the glasses are in the cupboard," Chris answered meekly.

Mark took out a glass from the cupboard to pour some water for Chris. He handed the glass to her and sat beside her. He watched her take several sips of water before telling her his story.

"First of all, I am assuming that your breakup has a lot to do with the heartache you are going through at this time, am I right?" Chris nodded her head in agreement.

"I cannot promise you that the tremendous pain you are experiencing now will go away tomorrow, but one thing I know for sure is that the heart is resilient and capable of recovering all in due time. Once you allow your heart and mind to heal, nothingcan stop your progress except you." Mark said with such sincerety. He paused for a moment to composed himself before telling his story.

"Let me share a personal story that happened a decade ago, but the memory is so vivid it seems like it happened only yesterday. I have never told anyone about this incident until now. My younger brother and I were like two peas in a pod almost our entire life. We were inseparable and did things together most of the time. He followed me wherever I went, which I did not mind because as an older brother, it was my way of keeping him in check and protecting him from any harm. We attended college together, and we were somewhat popular because we were party-goers. He met a beautiful gal and they started to hang out together. I missed our comradery, and I felt like I was losing my best friend. I did the most despicable act by stealing his girlfriend and made her fall in love with me. When he found out, he was completely devastated to the point of ending his life before I had a chance to confess to him that nothing intimate happened between us. It was because of my unforgivable actions that I lost a brother and my best friend. I enlisted in the military and became a Navy Seal. The rigorous training both mental and physical allowed me to take on any challenges or dangerous missions where the element of danger pale in comparison to the pain I felt for losing my brother and my best friend to this day. That probably explains why being a loner comes easily to me. It was not until last year when I went back for my mother's funeral when my aunt handed me some keepsakes that I found a letter to me from my brother. The gist of the letter was forgiveness, wishing me a happy life and someday honor him when I have a son by naming him Benjamin when he is bad or just Ben when he is good like his uncle. Ben will have to wait a long time, end of story." At that moment, Mark stood up from the stool and walked towards the kitchen window seemingly felt the thrust of the dagger going through his heart brought tears and grimace on his face. Mark had his back away from Chris to avoid seeing him go through his emotional pain. Chris slowly walked towards Mark and stood next to him. She gently strokes his back not saying a word. As they both looked out of the window, a hummingbird came to the window for a couple of seconds before flying away. They both looked at each other as though a divine intervention happened to them. Mark sensed that the letter from his younger brother, Ben, not only forgave him, but he released him from a lifetime punishment of self-inflicted bondage that he placed on himself, a confirmation from Ben to live his life to its fullest degree with much joy and happiness.

Chris finally stopped crying, attentively listening to every word of Mark's story. Hearing his story made her realize that her breakup may be dramatic and real, but it is nowhere close to the finality of losing a human life. Nonetheless, Mark's story inspired her to reevaluate and learn a lesson from her breakup. Chris reached out to hold both of Mark's hands to comfort him.

"Mark, I am so sorry for the loss of your brother. I cannot begin to imagine the pain you must be feeling. I can almost feel the pain that is in your heart." Chris said

Chris held his hands close to her lips to kiss them. She sincerely felt the hurt that Mark must be feeling. She put her arms around his shoulders to softly embrace him. They sat quietly while they held each other. Chris wanted so much to open up to Mark to tell him about her breakup, but she hesitated for a moment not knowing if she could trust another man again.

"Thank you for your compassion. It means a lot to me." Mark responded quietly

"In a short time that we have known each other, you have been a great comfort to me. I know I have big trust issues that I need to work on, but after you told me about your brother, I can tell you my story. You see, up until eight months ago, I was in a serious four-year relationship with a man who I thought was my soulmate. He was a young lawyer, smart, charming, impressionable, an aspiring politician. I met him at World-Wide Aeronautics Company during my job interview by the legal department in which he was one of the consulting lawyers for the company. Later, he told me he was impressed by my interview that he recommended me for the job, probably a line he uses to get girls to go out with him. My co-workers warned me early on that he is quite a ladies man. I was young and foolish, easily impressed and a naïve girl attracted to "bad boys." In my silly mind, I thought I could change him. Instead, he changed my thinking completely. I trusted him implicitly, and he could do no wrong during the four years we were together until I received a desperate phone call from another woman who told me she had been in a relationship with James for the last six months. The topper was when she told me she was carrying his child. When I gave him the opportunity to state his side, he called her a liar, just a stripper he met at a bachelor party, denied having any other relationship, etc. In the end, he finally admitted his guilt, but still wanted to be together. He made promises, vowed he would never do it again and showered me with expensive gifts to keep me. After all that, he made one big mistake. He gave me a beautiful diamond bracelet with initials engraved on the bracelet. Unfortunately, the initials were nowhere close to mine. Of course, he blamed the jeweler for making a mistake. It should have been a double red flag to me that a lawyer and a politician make lethal bedfellows - no integrity and no scruples. With that said, I have big issues with trusting another man. I know I have long ways to go to overcome that huge hurdle, but I am taking your advice to take one step at a time. "Chris responded positively.

"Chris, what you are going through right now may seem bleak, but if you allow your heart the time to heal one more time, I promise you those positive feelings will come back to you again. You must believe that you have it in you to get through those giant hurdles one hurdle at a time. Like your boss who has been like a father figure to you believes in you, I, too believe in you. I will be there every step of the way. On that note, it is time for me to go home so that you can get your beauty sleep and be more beautiful tomorrow if that is even possible. That did not sound right. I hope you know what I meant to say." Mark said it with a smile and slight embarrassment on his face.

"For the first time in a long time, I am looking forward to waking up in the morning to see what the new day brings me," Chris admitted.

Chris walked Mark to the door, hugged him and bid him good night. She went to bed that night, feeling the connection with Mark and it feels right, knowing she has a male friend that she can trust. She thought long and hard about the job offer. The encouragements she received from Mark gave her the push she needed to put in her application for the Director's job.

Reflecting back to their conversation, Mark determined to be a good friend to Chris and earn her trust. He sees that two distinct issues are going on, but in her mind, they are not mutually exclusive from each other, which may be clouding her decision on the job offer. Mark would be the first one to admit that he could not add any more sound advice to Chris other than what has already been said. Timing and her willingness to follow her heart and her good instincts will determine her recovery.

Sunday morning Chris received a call from Sandy, inviting her and Lorraine to have lunch at the New Greek restaurant just around the corner from the apartment complex. Chris agreed, so they planned to meet at eleven-thirty by the foot of the stairs nearest to Chris' unit. Sandy was hoping they would run into Mark and invite him to lunch.

Mark happened to be looking out his window and saw Chris standing at the foot of the stairs. He quickly came out to check out what she was doing out there.

"Hey there neighbor, what are you doing out here? Are you locked out of your apartment?" Mark asked

"Hi there, I am meeting Sandy and Lorraine for lunch. There is a new Greek restaurant around the corner that just opened." Chris responded. By then, both Sandy and Lorraine were walking up.

"Oh, yes, I was there last week. I have been thinking of taking you there. Let me know what you think of their food." Mark highly recommended the restaurant.

"Hello, ladies." Mark greeted Sandy and Lorraine

"Hey there, we are just about to try out the New Greek restaurant, would you like to come with us?" Sandy asked

"Perhaps, I can join you another time. Thank you for the offer. Let me know how you all liked the food. Enjoy your lunch." Mark commented as he walked towards the gym.

"Isn't he just a perfect creature?" Sandy commented

"Chris, what do you know about Mark?" Lorraine asked

"Not much, other than he is new here in Washington, no friends or families. He works for the U.S. Government as an independent contractor." Chris stated. She did not say any more to avoid any speculation or further questions on Mark.

"He is a bit mysterious would you agree Chris? I tried to get to know him the first time I met him, but he does not talk about himself much." Sandy commented

"I don't know much about him. He seems to be a very private individual. You know about my recent breakup that I am working through. Having any love interest is the farthest thing from my mind. I am sure he would not mind you ask him his status. He will probably be flattered." Chris answered honestly

After Chris, Lorraine, and Sandy ate their lunch; they decided to see a movie. Not far from the restaurant is a theater that shows old movies. At the time, they were showing "Sleepless in Seattle" with Tom Hanks and Meg Ryan. It is a romantic comedy about a widowed architect who has a son who calls a radio station to ask about wanting to find a wife for his dad for Christmas. A woman from New York happened to be listening to the radio station. It was the kind of movie that most women find romantic.

By the time Chris got home, it was shortly after five PM, just in time to go for a run. She saw Mark outside his apartment doing some stretches. She called out to Mark.

"Wait up; can I come along for the run? Let me just quickly change my clothes." Chris asked as she hurriedly went to her apartment.

"Sure, I will wait," Mark replied

Chris quickly changed into her jogging outfit. This time, she had a light jacket tied around her waist. When Mark saw her with a light coat, he just smiled. He remembered the rainstorm they encountered the first time they went for a run.

"Should I grab a jacket in case it rains?" Mark commented

Chris just smiled and said, "Let's just go."

"How was lunch?" Mark asked

"You were right, the food was excellent, and the service was good," Chris commented.

"What did you ladies do after lunch?" Mark asked

"We went to see an old movie "Sleepless in Seattle." Obviously, the movie continues to be popular locally even though it was first released back in 1993, starring Tom Hanks and Meg Ryan. Have you seen the movie?" Chris asked.

"Yes, as a matter of fact, I saw it recently on TV. The title caught my eye as I happened to be searching for something to watch. I saw the scene when the son, I think his name is Jonah, called on the talk show talking about his dad. I was caught listening in on the conversation between Dr. Laura and Jonah, how she sensitively and carefully answered the young boy's questions. Before I knew it, I sat through the entire movie and enjoyed it." Mark was not afraid to admit that he sat through a "chick" movie.

"We are getting close to the apartment complex. Would you like to stop at our famous coffee shop?" Chris asked

"That sounds like a good idea." Mark concurred

The outdoor mall in this "bedroom town" in Everett Washington comes to life on Saturday night with people shopping, trying out different restaurants, going to specialty shops or just getting together with friends. The line to order coffee at Starbucks was outside the door, no table available inside. It was a beautiful night in comparison to when the two of them went for a run the first time. Mark and Chris decided to sit by the fountain located in the center of the mall.

"I love the sound of the water trickling down on the fountain. It is soothing and calming, don't you think?" Chris commented.

"Yes, I would agree. What a difference tonight's weather with the rain storm we encountered the first time we went out to run." Mark remembered.

"I remember that was the day I told you about the job offer. Since that talk, you recognized that I have other issues that I am working on. You and I have experienced profound losses that have changed our lives. As a result of our life experiences, I feel a connection and a great friendship with you. I hope and pray that we both find that happiness in life and that we continue to be good friends.

"Thank you, that means a lot to me knowing that I have your friendship. Before I forget, I will be going away for another business trip for about ten days, starting this Wednesday. I hope to hear great news about your new job by the time I get back." Mark stated. He noticed that there was a change in Chris' facial expression as soon as he mentioned he was going to be away on a business trip.

"Oh, you're going to be away? Do you know where you are going this time?" Chris asked.

"I will be meeting up with my team in Denver, Colorado. I will know more once we meet up. Some of these guys I have not seen in a couple of years. We usually have a good time when we get together." Mark wanted to put Chris's mind at ease. Some of the stores began closing their doors. They started walking back to the apartment complex. When they reached the stairs, they hugged each other and said goodnight

The next day was Sunday morning. People were just waking up to a new day. Chris just stepped out of her apartment to go to church. Mark happened to be coming out of his apartment, carrying what looked like a sea pack full of laundry. They both ran into each other at the foot of the stairs.

"Good morning, Chris. You look lovely this morning." Mark greeted Chris

"Good morning. Thank you, kind sir, for the compliment. It looks like laundry day for you. I was just on my way to church." Chris responded with a smile.

"Oh, yes, it has been a long time since I have gone to church. Will you put in a kind word to the good Lord for me? Enjoy your day." Mark said

"I will. Have a good day." Chris said

On the way to church, Chris thought about inviting Mark for a home cook meal. After church, Chris decided to get some groceries and surprise him with dinner. By the time she got back to her apartment, she saw Sandy and Mark by the pool, sitting on a couple of lounge chairs seemingly having a good time talking and laughing. They had their backs to her unable to see when she walked up to her apartment. She proceeded to prepare dinner. About a half hour later, she heard Mark's door closed. Her curiosity made her listen intently to hear if Mark and Sandy continued their conversation at his apartment. Not hearing any sound from downstairs was worse than hearing voices. Chris felt some jealousy coming on, and her imagination began to play tricks on her mind. She thought long and hard about the sense of resentment she felt towards Mark. This could not possibly be real feelings since they were just friends. She needed to clear her head of these crazy thoughts, so she went for a quick run at the beach.

Mark had been inside his apartment folding his laundry, hoping that Chris would knock at the door to invite him to dinner. He can hear her light footsteps knowing that she was upstairs all this time. By the time he looked at his watch, it was after 6:00 PM. He thought about coming up to invite Chris to dinner, but he did not hear any footsteps from Chris' apartment. He took a shower and put the laundry away. It must have been shortly before 8:00 PM when he heard footsteps in the kitchen. Chris must have gone for a run.

The following Monday morning, Mark expected to run into Chris at the parking garage. He noticed that her car was already gone. When he got home, her parking stall was still empty. It was not until after seven PM when he heard Chris's door closed. He quickly put on his shoes and walked up the stairs. There was a light knock at her door. When she looked through the peephole, it was Mark.

"Hey, there, are you trying to avoid me?" Mark asked

"No, what makes you say that? I needed to do some research papers for my resume that has to be completed before my interview on Wednesday. I thought you wanted me to get the Director's job in HR. Would you like to come in?" Chris responded rather short.

Mark detected a tone in her voice that he has not heard before. "I will not stay long. I just wanted to make sure you are okay. Chris, is everything all right? I also wanted to ask if you would like to have dinner tomorrow night. I will be flying out Wednesday morning for a business trip that I mentioned to you."

Chris felt guilty about her selfish attitude. He does not deserve that kind of treatment when he has been so supportive and a good friend to her. She changed her tone immediately.

"Mark, I am sorry for my childish behavior. I think I am beginning to get nervous about this job interview. I know what I have to do and you have been there all along, giving me good advice, which I am grateful to have received. Yes, I would love to have dinner with you tomorrow night. If it is okay with you, I have a casserole to bake that I had planned to cook last Sunday. How about having dinner here tomorrow around 6:00 PM." Chris made the dinner offer.

"Did I miss a dinner date with you last Sunday? I am sorry if I forgot." Mark sounded concern about missing a dinner date with Chris.

"No, you did not miss a dinner date. When I came home from church, I saw you with Sandy by the pool. I assumed you already had plans." Chris admittedly said

"I would like to make a statement, but I hope you do not take wrongly. I know Sandy is a good friend of yours. She is a terrific woman, and I have no doubt she will make someone very happy. It is not me. With my line of work, it is not fair to share a life with someone where there are many unknowns. Being a loner is a perfect match for this kind of work I do. However, lately, I find myself thinking what it would be like to have that meaningful relationship, a loving family and a place to call home." Mark looked at Chris straight in the eyes as if he was sending her a message. Whether or not he intentionally directed it to

Chris, he quickly realized he would be adding more strain to her broken heart that she is trying to heal. He wanted to walk it back.

It caught Chris in an awkward moment, surprised by what Mark just said; she just looked away not knowing how to respond. The nervousness she felt seemed to have intensified as she tried to process the comment that Mark just stated.

"Would you like some tea?" Chris quickly asked

"No thank you. It is getting late and tomorrow is another work day. Besides, we have that dinner date tomorrow night. You haven't changed your mind, right?" Mark was trying to lighten things up after the comment he just dropped on Chris's lap.

Chris tossed and turned unable to sleep, thinking about the statement Mark made. It was nearing midnight, still staring at the ceiling. She got up to brew some tea. In her mind, is it possible Mark maybe considering having a traditional life and not wanting to be a loner anymore? Clearly, by his own admission, he likes being unattached, uncommitted and unknown. What changed his mind or is this only a fleeting moment, just some romantic ideas in his mind?

CHAPTER 5

SECOND DATE

The following day Mark stopped by the florist to get flowers for Chris. Out of the corner of his eye, he saw a beautiful orchid plant on display. It had a single stem of delicate, exquisite bloom of pure white flowers potted in a stunning crystal vase that reminded him of Chris. He just had to get it for her.

It was a few minutes after six when Mark walked up to Chris's apartment. He was holding the orchid plant below the peephole, so she could not see what he was carrying. The moment she opened the door she saw the beautiful orchid plant on his hands. Her eyes got so big with excitement that she put her arms around his shoulders to kiss him on the cheeks, then, quickly on the lips. In her excitement, she reacted purely innocent and natural, not much thought or planning behind it. She did not realize what she just did, which shocked Mark for a second and almost dropped the orchid plant. They both proceeded towards the kitchen/dining room area.

"Oh, Mark, the orchid plant is simply beautiful. Thank you…" her eyes started to well up as tears began to fall.

"You're welcome, why the tears?" Mark asked. He was pleasantly surprised especially the kiss he did not expect.

"That is what beauty does to me." Chris simply answered

"Where would you like me to place the orchid plant?" Mark politely asked

"I think it would be perfect on the dining table where we can keep an eye on it. The casserole is almost done, another five more minutes should do. What can I get you to drink? I have a bottle of wine that I have wanted to try. Would you like a glass or would you rather have something else to drink?" she asked

"Sure, I would like to try the wine. May I help you open the bottle?" he asked

"Yes, please, the wine glasses are already on the table. Take whichever seat you like," she said

Mark poured a small amount of wine into his glass just to sample the wine before he filled both glasses. He happened to notice a little write-up on the back label of the bottle but did not get a chance to read it. Mark commented how smooth and refreshing the red wine went down. The wine tasted fruity, slightly on the sweet side similar to a Riesling. Chris bought the bottle of wine during a wine tasting party with one of her neighbors. There has not been a special occasion to open the wine, until now. This particular wine caught her attention when the host mentioned that the wine came from a local vineyard in Crystal Cove Island located just one-hour ferry ride from Seattle. Additionally, the wines produced from this small vineyard used the fruit from the cherries grown from the small parcel of land on the island. The vineyard has won several awards which caught the attention of several vineyard owners from Napa, California.

"Eeemmm...the wine is good and refreshing. Where did you say the island of yours is located? It sounds like my kind of an island." Mark commented as he read the label on the back of the bottle.

— THE STORY: "There was a young couple who came separately to Crystal Cove Bay Island during a school field trip. When the couple met and fell in love on the island. They returned to the island to get married and build their house on the location where they first met. His wife's favorite flower happens to be the cherry blossom. He honored her by making a gazebo and planted rows and rows of cherry trees around the property. Since the husband's family owned a vineyard in Tuscany, Italy, he learned to make wines as a young boy. Instead of using grapes to make wines, he used the fruit from the cherry trees. During the harvest season, which is late summer around August and September, they would invite many of their neighbors to share the wines made from the previous harvest. The husband went to war in World War II, but he never came back. His wife patiently waited in the gazebo every day for the 6:00 PM ferry that would carry her husband home to her, until her death 55 years later. She donated the property to the City of Crystal Cove Island. The original house no longer exists, but the gazebo continued to stand tall through harsh wind and rain. The cherry trees remained steadfast and produced healthy harvest year after year. Several orchard owners throughout the world have tried to transplant or cultivate the cherry trees to plant in other parts of the world, but no one has been able to duplicate the trees outside Crystal Cove Island. It has baffled the horticulturist around the world that has attempted to grow the cherry trees elsewhere outside the island. The cherry trees on this island use the water from the natural springs and have never been sprayed or treated with any chemicals yet, they thrive and continue to produce bountiful cherry blossoms and fruits.

After Mark read the brief story on the back label of the wine bottle, it intrigued his interest in wanting to see the vineyard. He would like to take Chris to Crystal Cove Island for a day to explore the island and possibly end the day with a dinner at the vineyard. In the meantime, it looks like Chris just took out the casserole.

"I think the casserole is ready," she said

"Before we eat, let's have a toast to honor a great chef, not just another pretty face, but she can cook a mean casserole. Here is to you, my dear friend." Mark raised his glass and lightly tapped her glass.

"My turn here is to someone who is a good listener and great at giving excellent advice. He claims he can cook a steak, but he has yet to prove his claim of glory. I could only take him at his word that he can cook as he says. Have a pleasant and safe trip. Cheers to you..." Chris returned the compliment. They were both having a good time while they enjoyed their meal, laughing, joking and being flirtatious, not talking anything serious, just having fun.

"Chris, may I have a dance?" Mark asked

"Mark, there is no music. Would you like me to put on some music?" Chris quickly answered.

"Don't you hear the music? Besides, who needs music?" Mark stood up and extended his hand.

Chris followed suit and stood up. She took his hand, and they both started to dance. Having just finished a bottle of wine, they were both feeling mellow. Because of Chris's low tolerance for alcohol, she did not seem to mind Mark holding her close. Then, the clock struck midnight. Mark and Chris seemed to be caught in the moment that nothing mattered except two people slow dancing to the music playing in their minds.

"It is late. I should go. Chris, I don't want to leave you." Mark whispered in her ear.

"Sssshhh, the music is still playing." Chris maintained her hold. Mark did not want to let her go. After a few minutes, Chris looked up at Mark and said, "Thank you for the dance and a lovely evening."

"It has been a delightful night, not wanting it to end. I would be lying if I did not admit wanting to stay. I am guilty as charged with being a man with mortal thoughts and desires of being in the arms of a beautiful woman. Just my luck, she still has the heart of another man. It is with great respect for this desirable woman that I need to restrain my mortal wants and desires. On that note, I better go." Mark explained. Behind his mind is the reality that Chris is still mending a broken heart. He gently kissed her hand as they walked to the door.

"Mark, what are you trying to say?" Chris quickly asked. She is a bit dumbfounded by what Mark just said. Was he just flirting with her or caught in the web of being a little intoxicated?

"I should not have said what I just said, knowing your current situation. It must have been the combination of the wine and a delightful evening with a beautiful woman that triggered these crazy thoughts. I want us to remain good friends, and I hope I did not jeopardize our relationship. Please forgive my gibberish talk. I better quit before I put my other foot in my mouth. Good night, Chris." Mark was trying to take back what he sad to Chris, not wanting to lose her friendship. He went on to say, "I have to go now." Mark sadly said. He quickly kissed her forehead lovingly and walked out the door.

Neither one of them could sleep that night. The next thing she heard was Mark closing his door around 4:30 AM. Moreover, she wanted to see him once more to say goodbye, but all she could see where the brake lights as Mark drove away. She needed to get a couple of hours of sleep before she goes in for the job interview.

For having only a few hours of sleep, she did very well during the job interview. She was confident, focused and determined more than ever to take on the challenges and responsibilities of the Director of Human Resources. Her experience in business law and her impeccable resume coupled with her excellent work history impressed the panel of interviewers that she would be on the top list of the candidates for the job. The final selection by the board of experts and upper management will not be known for another week. Regardless of the outcome of the director's job, Chris discovered her true self throughout the process. She gained back her self-confidence as a young executive capable of "breaking the glass ceiling" in the corporate world, and more importantly, restoring her faith as a woman to hoping someday fall in love again. At that moment, a picture of Mark came to mind as she thought about the kind of man she would be lucky enough to have.

After several days of not seeing Mark around the apartment complex, she soon realized she was missing him. How was that possible when he has been gone only a couple of days. Whenever she sees the orchid plant, she will pause and recall their last night together when they danced to silent music playing in their head. Remembering that moment in time brought a smile on her face. Why was she behaving strangely when they were just good friends? There was no explanation. It needs to stop.

She called Sandy and Lorraine to see if they wanted to have dinner together. They both responded yes to Chris' invitation. After dinner, Sandy suggested they watch the Travel channel while they have coffee and dessert. The Travel channel was featuring Crystal Cove Bay as a vacation destination. It was only an hour ferry ride from Seattle. After they watched the show, Chris was convinced that it would be the next destination on her vacation wish list.

Friday afternoon when most people in Chris's office were already making plans for the weekend, her boss called her to come in his office. The people that were interviewed for the Director's job were going to be notified of whether or not they got the job. As she walked into his office and saw his facial expression, she concluded that she did not get the job. Here we go with the fatherly speech of encouragement.

"Hi, Chris, please have a seat. I just got the word from the upper management on the job offer, to be a Director. They were impressed by your resume and your job interview, but there is a late development planned for the Everett location that needs to be disclosed. The Federal EPA (Environmental-Protection-Agency) in agreement with the state of Washington created an important program to convert paper data into an online system, creating a paperless environment. They have chosen our company, World-Wide Aeronautics Company, to implement the program. There are enormous business tax benefits and financial gains, not to mention the publicity implications to be the model company for this highly sought- after project by other companies nationwide. The environmental implications alone to "save the planet" by sparing the trees benefits the entire world. The planning, designing, technological tools, training and the resources needed to implement the conversion, using best practices have all been done and paid for jointly by the EPA and Washington State. It would be just a matter of our company to provide the raw data. As the Director of HR in Everett, your team will be responsible for completing a near impossible project before April 30 of next year. Are you up to the challenge?"

"What? I thought you were going to tell me that I did not get the job." Chris was pleasantly surprised.

"Congratulations, Chris! This is not going to be an easy project, but the panel of interviewers made the right and smart choice. I have to ask you officially, do you accept the job? Is Everett your location of choice to work?" he asked

Getting the director's job and hearing the positive words from her boss and mentor confirmed that she made the right decision. Mark came to mind immediately, the validation she needed to listen and follow her heart. In a couple of days, Mark will be home to tell him the good news. She walked up to her boss to hug him as happy tears streamed down her face.

"Yes, I accept the job. I pledge to do my very best. Thank you for all your encouragement, advice, pep-talk, and most of all your vote of confidence. I will be forever grateful." Chris sincerely and proudly stated

"Good, then it is official that you have accepted the job offer. Congratulations, Chris! Go on and enjoy your weekend. Here are the compensation package and additional benefits. Go through it and jot down your questions. We will discuss them on Monday." her boss explained

When she went home, she paused for a moment at the foot of the stairs and said, "Mark, I got the job. I cannot wait until you come home so that we can celebrate my promotion. Please, come back to me." Chris pleaded.

It has been ten days since Mark has been gone. He was supposed to come back after ten days. Since it was a Saturday, Chris picked up some groceries for a meal in case Mark comes home late. She stayed close to home, not wanting to miss Mark or in case he calls. Occasionally, Chris would stare out the living room window to watch the cars coming into the apartment complex. The phone rang, and Chris ran up all excited to answer the phone, thinking it was Mark calling to let her know he was going to be late. It was Sandy calling.

"Hi, Chris, Lorraine and I were thinking about going to see a new movie at the theater. Would you like to go?" Sandy asked

"Yes, I think that might be a good idea. What time did you want to meet?" Chris asked

"Let's meet in about half hour, then, we can go get dinner before going to the theater," Sandy responded

The ladies met at Chris apartment. Sandy asked Chris about Mark. She responded by stating that he was on a business trip and due back soon. They proceeded to go to dinner and see a movie. It was about ten PM when the ladies returned. Chris noticed that Mark's apartment remained dark. He must have been detained somewhere.

The tenth, eleventh and twelfth day came and went no word from Mark. With each passing day, the intense feelings that Chris felt for Mark seemingly becoming more intense. Without any admission from Chris, she attributed the fierce feelings for Mark as infatuation or merely missing her interaction with Mark, nothing more. Besides, the last night she and Mark were together she admitted incapable of having a love interest because of her broken heart.

It has been nearly two weeks since Mark has been gone on a 10-day business trip. She remembered what Mark told her about having families back East. It is possible he may have visited his family on the way back from Everett? She hoped and prayed that would be the case.

Looking back at their first meeting in early June, they have been practically inseparable, except the first time Mark went on a 4-day business trip. They sustained great chemistry and strong connection from the start. Chris was going through life crisis in which she needed a trusted friend that can be fairly objective and not be afraid to voice their honest opinion on her issues. Enter Mark Ingram, who just moved in the apartment complex, new to the state of Washington, works for US Government immediately recognized that Chris seemed quiet, cautious, reserved, restless and unsociable at the time. Unaware of not knowing that Chris happened to be going through a broken heart from a 4-year relationship that she thought would result in having that fairy-tale ending. Never in a million years did she see an end coming that completely shattered her core beliefs and devastated her overall confidence in her judgment. Moreover, her greatest strength as a confident person began to slip away into oblivion and living a life of hopelessness.

However, Mark saw her differently, a "damsel in distressed." Beneath the fragile, shy, cautious, and almost stand-offish demeanor that Chris projected, he sees a special person with redeeming qualities just waiting to come out. After their initial meeting at the foot of the stairs confirmed his instincts were right on the money. Given the time and space to heal her heart and mind, she will regain her self-confidence and restore her self-worth more than ever. When that happens, Mark would be that dashing modern prince that rescued the damsel in distress. Where could her "prince" be?

Chris realized that each time she and Mark got together, they learned more about each other. Their friendship became stronger and more profound because they have great trust, honesty, sincerity, and respect for one another. Additionally, there is a natural comfort and ease of being around each other without putting a label on their friendship. Not knowing where Mark could be, she worried and missed him with each passing day. When she looked at her watch, the time flashed 5:45 PM, almost dinner time. Chris did not feel like having dinner, so she just sat at the dining table, admiring the orchid plant, remembering their last night together. She closed her eyes for a moment to capture the picture of them slow dancing to music playing in their minds. It quickly put a smile on her face.

CHAPTER 6

MARK'S HOMECOMING

Chris needed to clear her head and wanted a breath of fresh air. She decided to go for a run along the coastline of Puget Sound. She quickly put on her running shoes and planned to take the same route she and Mark had taken not so long ago. When she stepped outside her front door and just about to take the first step down the stairs, she saw someone standing at the bottom of the stairs, looking up at her with the biggest smile on their face. For a moment in time that seemed like an eternity, Chris thought she imagined seeing Mark, her "Rhett Butler." Waiting for Chris, his "Scarlett" to come down into his awaiting arms. It was like the classic scene from one of the timeless romantic novel ever written and made into a movie titled "Gone with the Wind." Still, Chris could not believe her eyes. She clasped her hands to her face in her amazement, trying to control her excitement upon seeing Mark standing there. She rushed down to his arms and buried her face in his chest, sobbing uncontrollably. He looked surprised by the reaction he received from Chris. He continued to hold her while stroking the back of her head. He decided to lift up her chin to look at her as he wiped the tears from her face, then, gently kissed her on the lips. He felt no resistance, nor, pulling away from him. Instead, she returned a passionate kiss while she continued to hold on to him ever so tightly. They could have stood at that spot all night until Mark whispered in her ear.

"We better go inside before we become the talk of the entire apartment complex." he quietly suggested.

Chris caught in the moment, full of excitement; she did not realize they were outside his apartment. When she finally pulled back, she noticed that Mark had a soft cast on his left leg. She immediately asked what happened.

"What happened to your leg?" she inquired

"Let's go inside my apartment, and I will tell you all about it. My crutches are inside because I did not want you to see me with them on and possibly scare you. I will need to lean on you for support." he requested

Mark put his right arm on her shoulders as they started to walk in the apartment. Chris carefully wrapped her arms around his waist for support. The soft cast provided support from his left foot to just above his knee, exposing only his toes. He sat on the couch so that his left leg could be extended. Going by Chris' reaction while they were outside his apartment, he hoped she would sit beside him on the couch. Not questioning the intent of the kiss from Chris, he held back to avoid talking about where their relationship was going. He gave her the time and space needed before putting a label on their friendship. Being inside Mark's apartment for the first time, she looked somewhat nervous. As she looked around to find a place to sit, his tidy and neat apartment surprised Chris. She attempted to start a conversation.

"Are you comfortable enough? Do you need any pillows to support your leg? How long will you have to wear the cast?" Chris asked questions in rapid succession, sounding anxious about being there.

"I am comfortable at the moment, but I am not sure if you are okay. Are you all right?" Mark politely asked

"Why shouldn't I be okay? I should be asking you that question." Chris quickly responded

"Chris, would you like to sit down? You are making me nervous," he said with a slight smile on his face.

"I am sorry. Can I get you something to drink or eat before I sit down?" Chris asked before taking a seat.

"Yes, I would like something to drink. In the fridge are some sodas.

Help yourself with the drinks. Please, grab one for me too." Mark requested. It will give Chris something to do to help her calm down.

Mark's unit was set up precisely like Chris', so she was familiar with her surroundings. She handed a drink to Mark as she sat down on the floor, next to Mark. She took sips from her drink, occasionally looking up at him waiting for him to settle on the couch. She calmly asked about what happened to his leg.

"I wish I had a heroic story to tell you, but the truth is I fell off the helicopter during an emergency landing. I did not know I had a broken ankle until I stood up to try to walk. Luckily, it was a clean break, no bone chips, so the recovery should be much faster. The soft cast is to stabilize the ankle and heal faster. They kept me in the hospital for several days until I can put twenty-five percent weights on the ankle. The hospital wanted me to stay another week, but I was anxious to get home. They could not hold me down, end of story." Mark stated. "Now, it is your turn." He added

"Are you hungry? You probably have not eaten dinner yet. How would you like I order a pizza for dinner?" Chris asked

"What a great idea. I am hungry for good Old Italian pizza. I think I have some beer in the refrigerator." Mark quickly responded

"Okay, let me just place the order. They will be delivering the order in about 30 minutes," she said

While Chris placed the order for a pizza, she had a couple of minutes to think about what she wanted to say to Mark. Now, that Mark is back, she tried to validate her strong feelings for Mark. Are her feelings real and sustaining or is she just caught in a fleeting moment? She also wanted to ask him what he meant by having a traditional relationship.

"Mark, we need to …" Chris started to say

"I wanted to …" Mark spoke at the same time as Chris was just about to say something. He stopped in mid-sentence to allow her to speak. "I am sorry; I didn't mean to interrupt you. What were you just about to say?" Mark asked

"It can wait, please continue with what you were about to say." Chris yield to Mark, she needed more time to gather her thoughts.

Chris sat herself down as Mark was about to say something when the doorbell rang. Their pizza order came just at the right time. They enjoyed sharing a meal together like old times, while they played cat and mouse with their endearing glances.

"I am glad to be home to the USA. There is no place I would rather be." Mark commented.

"Mark, are you ready for some good news? Do you remember the job offer for Director in HR?" Chris reminded Mark of the job offer he helped her apply.

"Of course, I have meant to ask you about it, but with all of the excitement of being home, I put it aside." he quickly answered

"I got the job as the new HR Director in Everett location, effective October 1. It will be officially announced during our staff meeting," she said with enthusiasm and excitement in her voice.

"Chris, I am so proud of you. Congratulations!" Mark would have given Chris a hug and a kiss, but he happened to be sitting down on the couch and could not stand up right away due to the cast.

"Thank you, Mark. I could not have gotten through the process without your guidance and your support. You gave me the confidence I needed to believe I could do the job. I will be forever grateful for helping me gain back my self-assurance." Chris meant every word she said to Mark.

Chris had more good news to share about the package deal that came with accepting the promotion. Since Chris already resides in Everett, she saved the company the expense of not having to move her. Instead, the company offered her a luxurious two-week paid vacation for two people, all expenses paid. The only condition attached to the offering that the vacation must be completed before October 1, the first day as the new Director. Considering the limited period when she could take the two-week vacation, Crystal Cove Island would be on the top of the list for the destination. To complete the dream vacation, Mark would be the ideal choice to be with her on this enchanted island. However, she must honestly answer some questions before she tells Mark about her vacation plan. Is she ready to start a relationship? How does she honestly feel about Mark? Is Mark ready to have a traditional life? How will he accept the invitation? There are a few questions that crossed Chris' mind. More importantly, she does not want to compromise their friendship in case it does not work out. Also, because she is unsure about her emotional issues, she has to be very clear about her intentions and expectations before they can go on this trip. On the other hand, she does not want to lead him on, not knowing what he meant about pursuing a traditional relationship. She cannot take a chance at seeking a romantic relationship so soon, not knowing for sure what her strong feelings are for Mark.

"Mark, part of the package included accepting the position in Everett is a paid vacation that I have to take before October 1. As soon as I start my new job, I may not have the time to take off because of the additional projects that must be completed before the end of the fiscal year, sometime before April 30 of next year," she said.

Chris looked at Mark to see his reaction. There was a look of sadness on his face as he tried to look away. Oh, how he would like to go on this vacation. He pretended to be excited for her sake.

"It sounds like a dream vacation. When will you be going on this trip and where are you going?" Mark commented quietly.

"Mark, before I answer your question I have to ask you a question. Sorry, I am having difficulty finding the right words to say." Chris paused for a moment to collect her thoughts. She went on to say, "Because of time constraint and not requiring too much planning on where to go on vacation; I opted to go to Crystal Cove Bay Island as soon as it could be arranged. Here is my question to you, how would you like to come with me to Crystal Cove? Before you answer, I have to be honest with you as to where my heart and mind are at this time. My heart is in the state of healing and in need of being stable. My mind is focused towards my new responsibilities at work, but it does not mean that is all I am thinking about. I must admit that if you had not come along to make me see the importance of putting a sense of order in my life, I am certain I would still be searching for answers. I am thankful for having your unconditional friendship when I needed it the most." Chris was very sincere when she admitted how vital he has been to her.

"Chris, first of all, I am profoundly honored by all the kind words directed to me. Secondly, you have given me too much credit for what you have accomplished by yourself. You are a confident, smart, beautiful, talented young woman who just experienced a setback. Now, you are beginning to make your way back from that experience with excellence. The future looks bright for you." Mark commented

"Thank you, Mark. That means a lot to me for you to say that." Chris had a concerned look that he was just about to decline the offer.

Mark must have seen the puzzled look on his face. He wanted to walk up to her to give her an answer, but because of his limited mobility, he could not stand up right away. He needed to make sure that Chris' sincerely meant to ask him to go on this vacation, not just an obligation to return the gratitude for the things he may have done for her.

"Chris, I would love to see this island of yours. I can promise you that nothing inappropriate will happen to you that would not be right. You have my word." Mark answered with a smile on his face. He spoke with sincerity and with great care.

"Is that a yes answer?" Chris asked with excitement.

"Of course, the answer is yes. When do we leave?" In his excitement, Mark forgot to give his answer.

"I just need to make the reservations and turn in my vacation request. It would only take a day or so. How about you? When would you know if you could go? How is your leg?" Chris responded

"Having just come back from a trip, I have an option to be off the rotation until my ankle is completely healed. I just have to notify my team within twenty-four hours, then, I am free to go. I think it will do my leg some good to get lots of walking. Luckily, it was a clean break. I am truly grateful for the offer, thank you." Mark said

"You are welcome. Then, it is settled." Chris was delighted.

There was a sense of innocence and naiveté from Chris, seemingly avoiding the consequences or risk involved if they find themselves pursuing taking their relationship beyond the friendship level. For Mark, he is torn between following his heart and confronting the reality that he may never have that traditional life that has eluded him in the past. Despite the tremendous challenges facing them, Mark agreed to take the challenge to see where it will lead them. He accepted the reality that this may be the only "alone time" he will ever have with Chris.

"I will make the arrangements in the morning and let you know when we can leave," Chris stated.

It was nearing midnight by the time Chris looked at her watch.

In her heart, she did not want to leave, but after telling Mark what is in her heart and mind, she has to remain faithful to herself. Having Mark back home safe and away from any danger filled her heart with happiness that could only be matched by his acceptance to go to Crystal Cove Bay Island.

"It is getting late. I should go and let you settle in from your trip. I have to go to the office tomorrow to put in my vacation request and notify my boss that I am taking some time off. I have to be back before our next staff meeting." Chris explained

"Of course, it has been a fun evening. Can we plan on having dinner tomorrow night?" Mark asked. He wanted so much to have Chris stay, but he understood her situation. He was glad to see her.

"Yes, let us plan on having dinner together here tomorrow night. I know it is difficult for you to come up the stairs, so I will bring dinner here. Will that be all right with you?" Chris asked

"It is perfectly fine with me. Let me walk you to the door." Mark was a little slow with having the cast on his leg. When they reached the door, Chris turned around to face Mark and gave him a long kiss before she ran up the stairs without saying a word. Mark had a big smile on his face while he stood by the door. He waited until he heard Chris closed her door before going in.

The following day, Chris went to the office to turn in her vacation request. She talked to her boss about the vacation package, wanting to be off ASAP. Her boss approved her request and told her to have a good time, knowing that when she starts her new job she will be working long hours and she might not be able to take as much time off. Chris was excited about her vacation with Mark. She made all the reservations, and they were scheduled to leave the following day on the 3:00 PM ferry ride to Crystal Cove Bay. She went home early so that she can tell Mark all about the trip. When she got close to her apartment, Sandy was standing in the doorway to Mark's unit knocking at his door. Because of the cast, Mark was unable to open his door right away.

"Hey, hi Chris, I was just about to invite you, Mark and Lorraine for a BBQ this evening, so that we can talk about the upcoming holidays. I've got all the fixing by the pool area." By that time, Mark came to the door and found Sandy and Chris by the foot of the stairs. Sandy greeted Mark.

"Hey, Mark, we were just about to have BBQ by the pool. Want to join us? Chris is the first person I saw, now, you. I am going to knock on Lorraine's door." Sandy walked over to Lorraine's unit, leaving Mark and Chris alone for a few minutes.

"What do you know about this BBQ event?" Mark asked Chris

"I did not know about the BBQ until a few minutes ago. I just got home and saw Sandy standing by your door. That is when she invited me to the BBQ. We might as well go along with her plan. What do you think?" Chris said

"If you are game, so am I. I was hoping we would have a quiet dinner together. Here she comes." Mark stated

"Lorraine will be joining us, and she will be bringing the wine coolers and drinks," Sandy said

"Do you need anything else? I think I have Caesar salad I can put together. Let me go get it." Chris quickly got the salad she prepared for her and Mark.

"Okay, that would be great. Let's all meet at the pool." Sandy walked towards the pool to get things started.

The girls were just setting up the table and started to put out the food and drinks. They stopped for a moment to notice that Mark had crutches under his arms as he ambled towards them.

"Oh, my goodness, what happened to your leg?" Sandy asked.

"What did you do to your leg?" Chris went along with the questioning even though she already heard the story. She pretended to be surprised, and she tried to ask Mark about his leg seriously.

"Well, ladies, I had a slight accident during my last trip a couple of weeks ago. We were playing a game of football when the accident happened. The good news was our team won the game, end of story. May I help with cooking the steaks? It is one of the few things I can handle." Mark claimed and modified the story for their protection. Of course, Chris knew the real story.

"I was hoping you would volunteer to handle the steaks, thanks, Mark," Sandy said

"By the way, where are Tom and Marie?" Chris asked

"They wanted me to let you guys know that they went to Florida this morning because Tom's mother had a bad fall and broke her hip. She is going to be okay, but she needed some assistance while recovering. Tom and Marie decided to be with her while she recovers. They wanted me to let you all know that they will likely stay in Florida after Thanksgiving and they will be back before Christmas." Sandy explained.

"I hope everything is all right. The steaks are ready. Let's eat." Mark announced.

During dinner, Sandy asked many questions directing them to Mark, almost ignoring Chris and Lorraine. She was interested in getting to know him. Since Mark was the newbie in their circle of friends, Sandy explained what their plans for the holidays, hoping he will be in town. It was apparent to Chris that Sandy was flirting with Mark. He did his best to get Lorraine and Chris to join in on the conversation. Finally, Lorraine came to the rescue.

"I have some good news to share. Do you remember my boyfriend Pete who is currently in the Middle East? He will be coming home, hopefully, before the holidays. He has served three consecutive tours in the Middle East. He is ready to come home. I completely agree with his decision." Lorraine shared the good news with her "extended family" in Everett.

"That is great news, Lorraine. Do you guys know what your plans are after he gets out?" Chris asked

"We talked about getting married a while back before he deployed to the Middle East. That is still in our plan, but we are not sure where we would be making our home. He wants to discuss it further when he gets back." Lorraine replied

"As a military veteran, I might be able to connect him with some people from the U.S. Government if he is interested in finding a job. I hope to meet him when he gets back from the Middle East." Mark suggested

"Mark, thank you. I will let him know." Lorraine responded right away.

"Just a word of advice from someone who has been there, Pete is a changed man. That is one of the major hazards of being in the war zone. While he adjusts to civilian life, he will need to decompress from the stress of being on the frontline. Also, give him as much space and time to adjust to a civilian life. Most of all, you will need to be patient and vigilant about the changes in his personality. He will require lots of TLC, which I am certain he will get from you." Mark gave Lorraine a big brother talk. Lorraine's eyes were welling up, so she came up to Mark to give him a hug to show her appreciation. Both Chris and Sandy did the same thing. The ladies were so touched by his brotherly advice to Lorraine that they gave him a group hug. Mark was surprised at the reaction he received from the ladies.

"I think this call for a special treat. I have ice cream in my freezer for this occasion. Let me just get it. I need to stretch out my leg anyway." Mark suggested

"He is going to make some girl very happy. He is one hell of a man, do you not think so? Sandy commented as Mark walked to his apartment.

"Yes, I couldn't agree with you more. He is a kind and sweet man. What do you think, Chris? " Lorraine agreed.

"So far, he has been a good neighbor and a gentleman. I am so glad to have him living downstairs. It is like night and day in comparison to the previous tenant." Chris commented knowing that Mark is more than just a friend.

"Do you think he may have a girlfriend or possibly a wife? I sure would like to pursue him. He is my kind of guy." Sandy admitted

Chris felt somewhat jealous of Sandy's questions. She was not sure how to respond to her comments. Saved by Mark, he just got back from getting the ice cream

"Ladies, the dessert has finally arrived. The choices are vanilla, chocolate or strawberry. Help yourself." Mark stated

They each had a Dove ice cream bar for dessert. Mark had to excuse himself shortly after so he can finish his packing. He made the excuse of having to put the ice cream back to his freezer. He thanks them all for the lovely dinner and the pleasure of their company. The ladies stuck around for a little while to just catch up. When Sandy started to bring up Mark's name, Chris thought it was time to go. Also, she needed to talk to Mark about their trip the following day. Before the girls departed, Chris told them that she is going away for several days on a business trip. Sandy decided to walk with Chris back to her unit, hoping to stop in and see Mark for a short visit. Sandy has been smitten by Mark since she met him. Chris certainly understood what Sandy must be feeling. She quickly ran upstairs to her unit and just allowed Sandy to do what she intended to do. She knocked on Mark's door.

"Hi, Mark, I just stopped by to see if you are okay. Can I get you anything?" Sandy asked

"Well, I certainly appreciate your thoughtfulness, but I was just about to jump in the shower. Thank you, for stopping by." Mark politely responded

"Would you like me to help you wrap your leg?" Sandy suggested

"I am okay. I have a big trash bag to slip on to cover the cast." Mark responded.

"Sounds good, I better go." Sandy complied

"Sandy, I wanted to thank you again for a great BBQ. Next time, it will be my turn to host a BBQ dinner, hopefully soon. Good night. Would you like me to walk you home?" Mark suggested even though he has a cast on his leg, a perfect gentleman.

"Thank you, Mark, but I will give you a pass this time because of your cast. Good night, Mark" Sandy said as she walked away.

Chris heard Mark's door close. She waited for about a half hour before she came downstairs. She looked around before knocking on Mark's door. He had been waiting for her. He quickly opened the door knowing that it would be Chris.

"You know that Sandy has a crush on you. I can certainly see how easily that can happen. You have all the credentials for a perfect mate. Do you know that?" Chris commented in a jealous tone.

"I am extremely flattered by your comment, especially coming from you. It is important to me that you know I made no effort to encourage or entertain whatever Sandy might be feeling for me. She is a lovely woman, and she will make someone very happy. I am not that person." Mark explained

"I know that. Please be kind and gentle with her when you let her go." Chris pleaded with Mark the let her down easy.

"She reminded me of my little sister who was somewhat of a tyrant with her boyfriends. She liked the chase, so she made them work for it, only to be dumped by her in the end. She finally met her match and to teach her a lesson he gave her a taste of her own medicine before he married her. I saw them both during my mother's funeral. I congratulated her husband for a job well done in taming her. They seemed very happy." Mark described his little sister to a tee.

"That is a cute story, lesson learned. Okay, before it gets any later, we are all set to leave for Crystal Cove Bay on the three PM ferry ride from Seattle. Since you still have your cast, I will drive and use my car. I thought that we would leave here around 10:00 AM when the majority of the people have gone to work. We can have a light lunch in Seattle before we get on the three PM ferry. What do you think?" Chris asked

"It sounds like a plan. Chris, I need to ask you again, do you have any other reservations or expectations that I should know about? It is not too late to back out from your offer." Mark gave her a second chance to back out.

"No, I am looking forward to this mini-vacation. It might be the only vacation I will have before I work long hours starting October first. Likewise, if you want to back out, here is your chance. Otherwise, we are set for tomorrow." Chris had a stern look. She wanted to make sure Mark was on the same page. Mark walked her to the door. He sensed a little hesitation from Chris, so he just pulled her gently towards him to kiss her on the forehead before she walked out the door

CHAPTER 7

CRYSTAL COVE ISLAND

The following morning they met in the parking garage to load up their bags. They drove to Seattle at the ferry landing and got their tickets for the three pm ferry ride to Crystal Cove Island. They had time to get lunch before boarding. It was a beautiful day in Seattle, sunny, light breeze, a perfect place to have lunch outside the restaurant, with the view of the water. Mark bought a couple of sandwiches and drinks for lunch as they sat outside, admiring the scenery.

They boarded the ferry as scheduled. They sat on the upper deck of the ship towards the front side and watched the cars boarding the ferry. Next to their seats was a magazine rack containing many brochures on things to do on the island, places to see, where to stay, restaurant lists, etc. Chris picked up a brochure on the Crystal Cove Island Vineyard, listed as one of the places to visit.

According to the brochure, the vineyard is approximately 3.7 miles from the downtown area, towards the hills overlooking the Crystal Cove Bay. As the story goes, a young couple met, fell in love and married on this lookout, where they built their home. The husband added a gazebo surrounded by rows of cherry trees. It was a hobby of his to make wine from the cherries and share the fruits of his labor with his neighbors. During springtime when the cheery-blossoms are in full bloom, they would host a picnic to celebrate the wines made from previous year's harvest. This tradition continued until he enlisted in the Army during World War II. His wife would enjoy her cup of tea at the gazebo while she waited to watch him arrive on the six pm ferry from Seattle. Then, the husband went to war. They wrote love letters, filled with hopes and plans for their future together. She continued to wait patiently for additional fifty-five more years for her husband that never came back from the war. In his honor, she donated fifty lampposts during the downtown renovation. The number fifty represented the number of pearls on a strand of necklace her husband gave to her on their wedding day. The lampposts used provided the lighting along the bay from the lighthouse to the end of the pier. At night, the rows of lamppost from the tip of the lighthouse to the end of the dock appear to be like a strand of pearls encircling the downtown area.

Today, the main house has been converted to a glass-house restaurant/vineyard which has a complete panoramic view of Crystal Cove Bay – perfect seating for dining or just enjoy a glass of wine or two made from the rows and rows of cherry trees growing just a few feet away from the house. As you enter the glass front door of the restaurant, you will cross a small bridge with a stream of water piped in from the bay running under the bridge before you are met by a maître d' to seat you. While you wait to be seated, you cannot miss the display of memoirs' honoring the couple pictured on an enormous portrait on the wall, surrounded by some pages from their love letters they wrote to each other while the husband served his country during the war. The final love letter written by his wife summarized their eternal love story, with an enclosed picture of an elderly woman, sitting in the gazebo late afternoon / early evening, seemingly running her fingers on a strand of pearl necklace she wore around her neck as she clutched her cup of tea with the other hand. Shortly before she died, she willed the entire property to Crystal Cove Island with just small requests. First, any profit from the vineyard will be used to maintain the upkeep of the property. Secondly, no fees of any kind will be charged for simple ceremonies, celebrations, photography, etc., after approval from the City of Crystal Cove Island.

By the time Chris finished reading the article, the ferry was just entering Crystal Cove Bay. The lighthouse from the distant served as a marker that they were approaching the channel into the Bay. Across the bay are hills of cedar trees providing the backdrop for beautiful homes and A-framed cabins? The sun was beaming down on the bay waters, creating a shimmering reflection of the sun that seems to be dancing on the surface of the water. The weather condition felt similar to Seattle. The closer you get to the ferry landing, the long pier leading up to what looks like the downtown area becomes more visible. There are taller buildings, not more than four stories high, closer to the downtown area. Near the pier landing, close to the beach seems likely where people go for a stroll, a run, ride a bike, meet friends, or sit at one of many benches just to look out the picturesque view of Crystal Cove Bay as you breathe in the subtly salty air.

When they finally arrived and docked at Crystal Cove Pier, Chris can see the Crystal Cove Inn, their temporary home for several days. The Inn was within walking distance from the pier, but they reserved a golf cart to use while on the island. Due to the narrow streets all around the island, golf cart seems to be the mode of transportation, with the exceptions of some small buses used for public transportation or tour buses. They picked up their bags and golf cart at the terminal for the short ride to the Inn. When they arrive in their room, the subtle scent of spices and lavender filled the room as they opened the door. There was a massive fireplace and a big king size bed, with lots of frilly pillows, matching comforters. The wallpapers and the window treatments were all nicely coordinated, creating comfortable country surroundings as though Martha Stewart put her personal touches to every detail in the entire room. It was merely inviting to just curl up in bed and look out to the spectacular view of the bay. Chris and Mark just looked at each other with amazement and the look of contentment at the room/suite they were given. They set their bags at the foot of the bed and decided to do some exploring around the Inn before it got dark. There was souvenir/coffee shop on every block, bake shop, restaurants, and boutique stores that surrounded the Inn. Since it was getting late in the day to explore the island, they walked towards the downtown area and just sat at one of the benches and watched the sunset hide behind the forest of cedar trees. Along the way, they met and talked to some of the locals that would greet them and start a conversation. Most of them were anglers that can talk about the "big fish" that got away. The others like talking about the history of the island. After their walk, they went back to the Inn to have dinner at the restaurant. Seeing Chris and Mark together, the manager sat them in a very cozy spot usually reserved for newlyweds or honeymooners. The food was excellent, you could not ask for a better seating area, and the service people were so hospitable. They walked up to their room and saw that the bed had been set up for "romantic interlude," complete with a bottle of champagne, two glasses, a bowl of strawberries and chocolates. The fireplace was lit up with a couple of logs.

"Pinch me and wake me up from this dream. I feel so safe and calm here. What do you think of this place?" Chris commented as she lay on the big bed.

"If this is heaven, I like it. I am so glad they handled the pillows. I was not sure how we were going to sleep with all the pillows on the bed. It is a lovely room indeed. I would not mind coming back here again." Mark agreed and was delighted with the room.

"Me, too, I want to come back here on my wedding day and every anniversary after that," Chris said aloud what she was thinking in front of Mark. She was in the moment and quickly changed the subject, hoping that Mark did not hear all of what she said. Mark pretended he did not hear what she said.

"Would you like to have some champagne and strawberries?" Mark asked

"That would be a lovely way to celebrate our arrival at this enchanted island. Yes, I would love a glass of champagne, please." Chris answered

"Mark opened the bottle of champagne without spilling any of the bubbles and with a small pop. Chris happened to be looking out of the big window when Mark brought her glass to her and said, "Here you go, my lady. Let us toast to a perfect day and hope more days like today to come. Cheers…"

"Cheers, to you, kind sir. I am glad you are here." Chris commented with a smile.

"I am glad to be here. Thank you again for sharing your island with me. What are we doing tomorrow?" Mark asked. He intends to keep his word that nothing inappropriate will happen to Chris.

"I thought we would wake up early so that we can do some exploring.

Would you like to go to the vineyard lookout? During the ferry ride, I read about the vineyard. What an inspiring love story. I would also like to bring back some wine from the vineyard." Chris gladly responded.

"I am going to get something to drink at the gift shop. Do you need anything?" Mark asked. He wanted to give Chris some privacy before they go to bed. He had no illusions, nor, expectations anything was going to happen between them even though they will be sharing a bed together. When he got back, Chris was already under the covers, wearing a skin tone, spaghetti strap nightgown. As he got closer, Chris pulled the sheets over her shoulders. The bed was a king size, which dwarfed Chris as she was lying on one side of the bed. She was trying to look the opposite direction as Mark started to take off his shirt.

"I must warn you; I do not own any pj's. I sleep in my birthday suit only. They say it is healthier to sleep that way. I have adopted that theory for a long time. You have my word that nothing is going to happen to you as I stated before. You can put as much pillow between us to avoid any crossover. I will not be offended. So, if you want to turn away before I get in bed, now, is the time." Mark warned her.

"I am turning away. I do not need the pillows between us unless you do not trust me. This bed is so big I feel like I am in Canada and you are in the US. Can we get a little closer, an arm's length from each other?" Chris requested.

They both started moving towards the center of the bed. Mark stated, "Is this close enough? You tell me when you think you are at a comfortable distance."

"Thank you…good night," she said it in her sweet voice.

"Good night, Chris," he responded

After a few minutes, a sweet little voice said, "Mark, are you asleep?"

"Yes, I am trying to, but someone cannot seem to fall asleep." Mark turned towards Chris to hear what she had to say. "Do you want to wake up early tomorrow?" he asked.

"Can we talk for a few minutes? I have a lot on my mind, mostly having to do with you. You have done so much for me in gaining back my self- confidence and restoring my faith to become a complete person. I know I have a long ways to go, but I know now that is where I want to be my own person, again. All I could hope for is your continued support and patience in order for me to get through this broken heart and be a complete person again. You also said that there is more I need to know about you. Mark, I do not want to be hurt again, but if you already know what you want and it does not include me in your life, please let me go as soon as possible." Chris pleaded

"Oh, Chris that would be the last thing I want to do, and that is to lose you. Never in my wildest dream did I think I would meet someone like you. You make me want to feel those natural emotions that I have learned to suppress because of some decisions I made in the past. One of them was I made a pact with the devil long ago, not knowing that someday it will haunt me. It is only fair to tell you what you need to know about me. I have been a loner since I lost my brother. Perhaps, it was my way of self-punishment for what I have done. Without getting too specific and I hope not too many questions from you that I cannot answer, there is more I need to tell you." Mark said

"What is it, Mark?" Chris said with great concern in her voice

"Do you remember early on when you asked about my line of work and what brought me to your "sleepy town" of Everett, Washington? You politely asked if I were a spy or a secret agent on a covert mission. Your instinct was right on as if you knew all along what I did for a living. For our protection, I cannot say any more than what I just told you. I must admit that being here in Everett was no accident. My cover was exposed; therefore, I had to disappear for a while, so here I am. Until such time that it is safe, this is the extent of my existence. As a loner, you learn to accept loneliness, separation, isolation and uncertain future as a way of life. This is not the life I had envisioned for you. If given a hard choice to give you up to save your life, I will choose your life. This is as far as I think I can discuss this matter knowing that you have enough on your plate unless you want to go on." Mark hesitated for a moment to give Chris a chance to respond.

Chris sat up on the bed, not knowing what to say. Mark sat up without saying a word and just looked at Chris who was just looking out towards the big window. She had to quickly rationalize and make a choice for what she wants in her life. She only realized at that moment she wants a life with Mark no matter whatever length of time they are destined to be together. Her heart and mind agree that a life without

Mark is not an option. She bravely faced Mark and nodded her head as if she gave him the okay to say what was on his mind.

"Chris, I have very strong feelings for you that I am willing to admit. I want to be the only man in your life, to be in an exclusive romantic relationship with you, nothing halfway or on a trial basis. We either go all the way without any hesitation. If you tell me to wait, I will wait until you know for sure how you feel. As difficult for me to say and accept your decision to leave you, I will go as soon as possible. There, I said it." Mark meant every word he said.

"Is that how you really feel? We are headed to an unknown territory. I am scared." Chris admitted with some sadness

"I know. I am asking too much." Mark sees the fear in Chris' eyes, but also hears a sense of hope in her voice. He quickly added, "There is no question in my mind how I feel about you. I cringe at the thought of seeing you in the arms of another man. I do not expect you to be where I am at this moment, but I want you to be there when you feel what I am feeling." Mark let it all out, not holding back, wanting to know where their relationship is going.

"Will you hold me?" Chris asked

"With what I admitted to you, I cannot just hold you. I want to make love to you. This, silky nightgown has to go. I do not want anything between us but just our skin to skin." Mark told Chris what he wanted. He waited to see what she was going to do.

Chris started to remove her nightgown, her way of telling Mark she desires the same. Her heart is pounding so hard in anticipation; Mark asked her again if she was sure about this. She kissed him on the lips so tenderly. Mark had been waiting for this moment. They made love for the first time that night, so passionately and intently. He held her so lovingly and tightly that nothing could come between them.

They both slept peacefully like a baby, so much for waking up early to explore the island. They barely made it to the group breakfast, holding hands and exchanging endearing glances, with big grins on their faces. As they were about to leave the Inn, Chris stopped to kiss Mark.

"Mark, I do not want to leave this island. Can we just stay here forever?" She said it lovingly.

"I know what you mean. We have a few more days to explore the island and see what it has to offer." Mark said as lovingly as he passionately kissed her.

They joined the group for the usual breakfast celebration. The owner of the Inn led the group in a small prayer as the people who gathered around the table joined in. After breakfast, people went for walks, rode the golf carts, or just sat on benches to share stories.

CHAPTER 8

FALLING IN LOVE AND THE VOW

Mark and Chris decided to explore the island in their golf cart. There was only one main road on the island, so you could not get lost. If you do get lost, there are many friendly people to ask for directions. They stopped along the way to admire the view, shop, have a snack, or just bask in the sun. No one was rushed or hurried. People were so friendly as though you were one of the locals. Also, not too far from town was the lighthouse. Mark and Chris checked it out and walked up to the top of the lighthouse. Just below the lighthouse was a small mission/church house, nestled close to the water. They walked in, and there was a man in front of the altar kneeling with his hands clasped together praying. Mark and Chris sat a couple of pews behind the man. When he finished his prayers, he turned around and walked over to them.

"Good morning. How may I help you?" asked the man.

"We saw the chapel from the top of the lighthouse and just wanted to come inside," Mark answered

"Bless you, my children." The elderly man placed a sign of the cross on their forehead. He added, "If you would like to renew your vows and receive God's blessings, we can walk up to the altar and have the ceremony.

Somewhat embarrassed, Mark said they were not married. The elderly man asked if they would like to declare their love for one another. Chris and Mark can only stare into each other's eyes, then, in a few seconds they both let out a smile of contentment. They both must have realized that they have fallen in love and there is nothing more they would rather do than to declare their love for one another in front of God. Mark lifted Chris' hands to kiss them before walking up to the altar. The elderly man happened to be lighting the candles and started his prayers. Mark turned to Chris and said, "Chris, would you do me the honor of marrying me and being my partner in life forever?"

"Mark, are you sure about this?" Chris asked, but she saw the loving look in his eyes that she knew in her heart he loves her. She answered, "Yes, I will marry you." Chris had tears in her eyes as Mark held her closer to him just touching her face tenderly to wipe the tears.

The elderly man stood up to face both Chris and Mark. He said a small prayer, then, he pronounced them, "man and wife." He asked them to sign a piece of paper. After they signed the paper, Mark and Chris continued to hold each other's hands, staring into each other's eyes and kissed each other in front of the altar, unaware that the elderly man has gone. Not knowing the authenticity of the piece of paper they just signed, they accepted the blessing from God. The document had the heading of "Declaration of Love" and the seal of Washington State, a straightforward document like the ceremony. Other inscriptions were added by the elderly man such as, "I, *Mark Ingram,* take you, *Chris Jensen,* as *my partner in life, so help me God. Similarly, I Chris Jensen, take you, Mark Ingram, as my partner in life, so help me God.*" Nowhere does the word license appear on the document. They could not help but laugh at the whole thing, thinking that the elder must be an impostor and that they got pranked, They took the piece of paper anyway as a souvenir of their small ceremony, not sure how authentic or legal the document represents.

"Chris, before we go I need to ask you to keep this ceremony and our relationship a secret for our protection and until it is safe. Regardless of the validity of the document, I know what I feel in my heart is real. More than ever, we will need to be discreet about when or where we can be together. There might come a time when we both have to deny knowing anything about each other except just being neighbors, nothing more. Do you think you can handle that? This is a very serious matter and just as important to us to be vigilant from here on in order to stay safe." Mark was explicit in his instructions.

"Yes, I understand," Chris said it quietly

Before Mark and Chris left the small chapel, they made a pact to keep their relationship a secret for their safety and sealed it with a kiss. Despite the legality of the document they both signed, the vows they made to each other in front of God were genuine, sincere and embedded in their heart. They walked in as ordinary couple who has just fallen in love. Now, they are walking out symbolically as one, a "man and wife."

Mark and Chris walked outside the small chapel holding hands and smiling at each other, stopping only to kiss. With no destination in mind or on any rush to be somewhere, they got on their golf cart, sat close to each other as Chris rested her head on his shoulder and got back on the main road. Mark saw a sign to the Crystal Cove Island vineyard and the Glass House restaurant were only 3.2 miles away. They were excited to see the vineyard and the restaurant finally.

From the main road, a large sign pointed towards the sites for the vineyard look out. Mark and Chris took the turnoff to a narrow street, lined with cedar trees, leading up to the top of the hill. The second you pass the last cedar tree at the top, the sky seemed to open up to a spectacular view of Crystal Cove Bay, full view of the lighthouse, downtown area, the marina, the pier, Crystal Cove Inn. As soon as they parked the golf cart, they took the pathway that meanders through the rows and rows of cherry trees creating a pleasant stroll towards the gazebo where the view just astounds you. Mark and Chris stood inside the gazebo, looking out at the expansive view of the Bay as Mark pointed out some of the sites they stopped along the way. He took her hand and gently kissed it as if to say, *"I am so lucky to be here with you."* She looked at him lovingly as she responded in her mind, *"...so happy you are here with me."*

Further up the property, about twenty yards away, you can see the Glass House restaurant /tasting room that is shaped like a figure eight or if you look at it on a different angle the figure eight appears to be a sign of infinity. The entrance door, conveniently located in the middle of the figure eight, which opens up to a foyer where you are greeted by a very friendly maître d'. Standing at the foyer, just on the opposite side of the podium where you are greeted by the maître d', hangs a portrait of the famous couple on their wedding day as though they are welcoming you to their home. The wall of memorabilia honoring the legendary couple can be seen in travel guides, magazines, books, etc.

Since it was almost noon, Mark and Chris intended to have lunch at the Glass House restaurant. Because of its popularity, they would have to wait about thirty minutes to be seated. Chris decided to take a closer look at the portrait of the legendary couple. Off to the right of the portrait, the final love letter written to her husband before her passing included a picture of an elderly woman wearing a silk cherry blossom print dress and a strand of pearl necklace, standing inside the gazebo seemingly looking towards the pier. Chris began to read the letter only to pause for a moment to dry her eyes with a handkerchief. She felt the passion and the intensity of their love for each other, similar to what is happening between her and Mark. Chris went back to where Mark waited for her. She took his hand and gave it a squeeze as she smiled at him.

The maître d' came to get them to be seated. They walked over the small bridge with streaming water underneath the bridge being pumped in from Crystal Cove Bay. There are two steps up to the upper level to the restaurant for fine dining, a perfect place to dine and have a bird's eye view of the island from the gateway channel to the entire length of Crystal Cove Bay. The lower level takes you to the wine cellar, where you can enjoy samples of wines made from the vineyard or sits by the window, looking at the picturesque scenery the lighthouse to the marina. The combination of the sound coming from the stream of water running between the restaurant and the wine cellar, and the remarkable view of Crystal Cove Bay just take your breath away. The maître d' seated them next to the seamless glass wall so that they have an obstructed view of the bay. When the server brought their glass of wine, they were both speechless, unable to find the appropriate words to describe the ambiance that they were both experiencing. The endearing looks they cast on each other the entire time says it all.

"Chris, thank you, for our time together that I will never forget," Mark said wanting to kiss her, instead, sent her a distant kiss.

"You just captured my thoughts. I could stay here forever," she added

After they had their meal and enjoyed a glass of wine, they sat side by side to admire the view of Crystal Cove Bay. Feeling the effect of the glass of wine, Chris snuggled up to Mark to kiss him gently and lovingly.

"Isn't this a gorgeous place to enjoy a cup of tea and just look out into the unforgettable view of the Bay?" Chris commented

"Yes, I do. I am glad we made the stop. Should we get a couple of bottles of wine?" Mark asked. Chris nodded her head in agreement.

After they purchased a couple of bottles of wine from the wine cellar, they started their drive back to the downtown area so that they can walk around to check out some of the shops. Some of the stores were beginning to put out the decorations early in anticipation of the upcoming Thanksgiving thru Christmas holidays. They sat at one of the benches facing the ferry landing. The sun setting behind the hills provided the spectacular view of the bay as the reflections off the fifty lamp post that lined the pier shimmering on the surface of the bay water. Chris rested her head on Mark's shoulder as he leaned his head into her while holding her hand.

"What is it about this island that gives you peace and tranquility down to your core?" Chris commented. She went on to say, "The peaceful surroundings, the simplicity of life, friendly people and the cleanliness of the island, makes you wonder, why are not there more towns like Crystal Cove? I think I can live here forever."

"I get what you mean. The world would be a better place if people learned to live harmoniously and tolerate the diversity that people are different, color blind like the people here in Crystal Cove Bay." Mark said

"Wow! You just made a very profound statement on humanity. I totally agree with your statement. There would be no casualties of war. It has been a lovely day." Chris was touched by what Mark just said.

"We can probably sit here all night but are you not getting hungry? We can have dinner at the Inn and discuss our plans for tomorrow. What do you want to do tomorrow? Did you want to go back to any particular spot we have been or should we take the opposite direction we took today? According to some people, there are fishing villages and mostly residential community on the other side of the island. There are lots of eating places for seafood. It is highly recommended to stop for lunch at the Crab Cooker R Us; a must experience eating-place. What do you think?" Mark asked.

"I like that idea of taking the opposite direction. While we are there, just for grins, I would like to check out what a million dollar buys in the way of a real estate on this island. I could only dream about it." Chris said curiously.

"Do you think you could live here all year round?" he asked

"It would be fun trying. It is a place where you could get lost from the rest of the world, and no one would find you. Do you not think so? Just about all the people we have met so far are friendly and welcoming. They make you feel as if you have known them for a long time. I find it contagious, having a good and positive attitude in your daily life. People are right down accepting of others. It would be easy to blend in if you want a new start in life." She was making an observation

"Speaking of starting a new life, last night we took our friendship to a different level, changing the course of our relationship. Now, we need to be realistic about how we intend to be discreet and more importantly, to give you a traditional, normal loving relationship if that is even possible. Have I told you how brave and courageous you are for taking on such a challenge?" Mark said proudly

"Mark, hear me out for a minute. I have never been this happy in all of my twenty-eight years than I feel at this moment and it is all because of you. It was not so long ago that I merely exist and could not make heads or tails on what I wanted to do with my life. By the grace of God, you came just in time and saved me from drowning in self-destruction. You believed in me and stuck by my side all the way. You are the reason for my happiness. If it is our destiny to be together only for a short time, I am willing to accept that small measured of time than no time at all. I want us to cherish our happiness together while we are here on this enchanted island." Chris had to turn away as she cried uncontrollably.

"You are right. I am sorry to have brought it up. Let us enjoy our time together while we are here. It will never happen again as long as we are together on this magical island." He put his arms around her to hug her.

She composed herself to complete her thought by saying, "I know we have to eventually talk about the precautionary steps we have to take for our safety."

"It has been an enjoyable day. Should we go back to the Inn to get cleaned up before dinner?" Mark quickly changed the subject.

"Yes, it has been the most memorable vacation I have ever gone to in all my life, so far. I am amazed that such a place exists and it is only an hour ferry ride from Seattle. I hope to return to this island after completion of the project due before the end of a fiscal year, around April 30th and when things quiet down in the Everett location." Chris stated her heartfelt impression on Crystal Cove Bay.

"Wow, it seems like a long time. I know you mentioned having to work long hours to complete the project. Will I be seeing you at all during this time? I know it sounds selfish, but I am worried about you having to work long hours for several months." Mark showed genuine concern

"What a sweet thing to say. That means a lot to me to hear that from you. I will be home every night, except possibly two or three short trips to South Carolina for a joint meeting. Also, around Christmas time, the company will be closed for a week. We can plan to be here on the island at that time. I promise." Chris said to ease Mark's concern.

"I will hold you to that promise." Mark sounded serious.

"Speaking of promises, I will not ask you any more questions about your line of work. I get it. Will you promise me that you will always return to me forever?" Chris asked with such sincerity that Mark cannot say no.

Mark walked up to Chris to look into her eyes before he responded. He said, "I promise to return to you in person or spirit." Mark gently kissed her and held her a tightly not wanting to let go. They started walking back to their hotel suite.

Chris picked up a couple of items in her luggage before going in to freshen up. Mark happened to be looking out of the big window when he noticed a hot tub out on the terrace. The steam and vapors coming from the hot tub make you want to jump in.

"Chris, come here. How would you like to try out the hot tub just outside the terrace? Did you bring any swimsuit?" He asked.

"For a man who likes to sleep in their birthday suit, now, you are being modest. No, I did not bring a swimsuit." She was teasing him.

"I was thinking of you. Who needs a swimsuit? No one can see you unless a ferry boat mistakenly misses the dock. Otherwise, I think we can be risqué and go skinny-dipping." Mark suggested

"We might want to check it out before we get risqué. I would not want to get risqué and become the main attraction." She replied

They looked around the terrace to see how much can people see from the waterfront, not much at all. Whoever designed and built Crystal Cove Inn cleverly thought out every possible means to ensure privacy on any of the rental units. The Inn backs into the vast waterways entering the town of Crystal Cove. It was safe to be risqué in the hot tub. They both went in the hot tub in their "birthday suits." Mark went in first and helped Chris get in. The temperature of the water must have been around eighty degrees. She swam to him, and he wrapped his arms around her as they watched the sunset over the calm water of Crystal Cove Bay. As their bodies intertwined, the spectacular view of the sunset provided the perfect backdrop to the steamy passion happening between them.

"Are you getting hungry?" asked Mark

"Eeemmm, I can stay here all night. I will probably look like a prune by morning. Yeah, let us get dinner." Chris was agreeable.

They started to get out of the hot tub when Mark asked, "Do you still have the piece of paper we signed at the small chapel?"

"Yes, I do. It is on top of the dresser, next to my purse, why?" asked Chris.

Mark replied, "I wanted to check with the local authorities, just for grins. The document looks real. It has the seal of the State of Washington. I was just curious."

"You know I think we got ahead of ourselves by doing what we did. I want you to know that I am not going to hold it against you whatever that piece of paper represents. I thought it was just a prank. Didn't you think it was some sort of a prank to entertain the tourist that goes there?" In her mind she knew what was in her heart, but Chris did not take the ceremony seriously.

"Oh, Chris, I am surprised you said that. I, too, thought the whole thing was a setup to humor the tourist, but I know in my heart the vows I made came from my heart. You didn't think it was genuine?" Mark asked

"I was expecting Candid Camera to jump out from the bushes to say, "Smile, you are on Candid Camera and just been pranked. I thought it was fun while we made the pledges." Chris sounded skeptical

"I thought it was real, but now that you said it I thought it might be too good to be true. Let us get on with dinner. I am starving, aren't you?" Mark commented

While waiting to be seated at the restaurant, Mark and Chris were holding hands, staring endearingly at each other with sweet smiles on their face. The maitre d' must have thought they were honeymooners. He seated them near the window and close to the fireplace where it was warm and cozy. As a complimentary from the Inn, the maitre d' brought them champagne and strawberries for starters. What a way to end this day Mark and Chris were simply delighted and appreciated the gifts compliments of the Crystal Cove Inn. The memories they made today will forever be in their hearts for as long as they live. They ended the day with a toast of champagne to their future together as husband and wife, honoring the vows they made before God at the small chapel by the lighthouse.

CHAPTER 9

THE BLUE HOUSE

The following morning they rode the golf cart to the other side of the island where the local population mostly resides and fishing villages can be found. Just about every angler they met would talk about the "big catch" that got away or some historians that never seems to run out of stories to share with others. Mark and Chris looked into some real estate properties for sale. They were right; the properties were in the millions. Along the way, they saw a cute blue house with a white picket fence that was having an open house. Just for grins, they went in and saw how beautifully they decorated the house. To make the home saleable, most realtors would bake freshly made pies or cookies for the aromatic effect on the house. The realtor agent's desk happened to be in the kitchen. He greeted them and handed a freshly baked cookies and a brochure on the house. As they walked through each room, they can see themselves living there, making only minor changes. The home has country flair, with built-in modern appliances and utilizing every space efficiently both inside and outside. There were some excitements in their voices, especially Chris when they asked the realtor questions about the house. It was getting late in the day; the realtor agent invited them to stay and have some apple pie and coffee. It was hard to refuse, so they stayed and enjoyed the treats. When they started back to the Inn, all they could talk about was the blue house, what a dream it would be to own such a home.

When they got back to their room, it was almost time to meet up with some of the tourist they have met on the island. They would meet for dessert and coffee and just talk about how they spent their day on the island. The apple pie and coffee they had at the blue house kept them from going out. Instead, they saw a bowl of strawberries chilling in ice, a bottle of champagne, assorted cheese and crackers, and a box of Godiva chocolates. They looked at each other with a big smile.

"What do you say we have a picnic in front of the fireplace? I will lay out the blanket and throw in a couple of logs of wood." Mark suggested

"I will bring the strawberries and the rest of the treats while you bring over the glasses and the champagne bucket." Chris set up a small picnic in front of the fireplace.

Mark threw a couple of fire logs before sitting in front of Chris, facing her while she held two glasses of champagne. They romantically shared succulent strawberries, each taking bites of the fruit until their lips met. The effects of the bubbly champagne and the sweet berries heighten their passion for one another. They made love, and both fell asleep on the floor.

Chris woke up early dawn and just stared at Mark as he lay asleep. She quietly got up and sat in front of the big picture window to watch the sunrise peeking in the sky. Mark got up and noticed that Chris was not next to him. He saw her by the window just staring aimlessly at Crystal Cove Bay. He sat behind her and put his arms around her.

"What are you doing here by yourself? You seem in deep thoughts. Do you want to share your thoughts with me?" Mark whispered in her ear.

Chris turned to face Mark and said, "I don't want to leave this island without telling you, I love you with all my heart."

"Oh, Chris, I have wanted to hear that from you for so long. I love you too." Mark kissed her passionately for a long time. Just give me one year to finish my commitment, and I will be yours forever. Can you promise to hang on for that length of time?" Mark wanted a commitment. He was still holding Chris as she nodded her head in agreement. Mark carried her to the bed and held her lovingly and intently.

When Chris woke up later in the morning, she found a loving note from Mark next to her pillow. It just said, "My Love, I will be back shortly. I love you, Mark." They have a couple of days to go before going back to Everett. She decided to take a shower and got ready. By the time she finished her shower, she saw Mark standing by the window, drinking a cup of coffee. She put on her robe and walked behind him to put her arms around his waist. He turned around to give her a passionate kiss. She took a sip of his coffee.

"Where did you go?" Chris asked

"I didn't want to wake you this morning. You looked so peaceful just lying there. May I pour you a cup of coffee? I did not know what guilty pleasures you wanted with your coffee, so I asked the barista to pack up what they had. I hope I covered all the possibilities, my love." Mark said lovingly

"What were you up to this morning?" Chris asked again

"I went to the city hall, forgetting that it was Sunday. I wanted to authenticate the paper we got from the mission chapel." Mark answered

"Were you having second thoughts? As I said, not to worry, I will not hold it against you. I know what I feel in my heart." Chris replied without any hesitation.

"I want you to believe it is real as I do. It will live in my heart and my mind for as long as I live." Mark declared his beliefs

"Mark, I sound like a broken record, not wanting to leave this island. I feel you the most being in this island" Chris lovingly said

"I feel the same way. We will come back here again, I know it. Just give me one year, and we can have the traditional life that I could only dream about. Now, having you in my life, I can see a real future. When we get back to the mainland, we need to be extra careful and not make any sudden changes for our safety." Mark needs to make that critical note.

They spent the next couple of days exploring the island. They went for a run at the marina, hiked some of the recommended trails in the hillside. There were historical tours they took of notable Victorian homes on the island. On their last day, they visited the vineyard to have a glass of wine to toast the unforgettable memories they made on the island. They cherished their time together as they looked out at Crystal Bay.

The look of sadness in Chris' face and the thought of leaving the island in a few hours brought tears in her eyes as she was packing her luggage,

"Mark, I need to ask you if I can have the shirt you wore yesterday? I would like to have a keepsake from you." Chris asked

"It is dirty. Would you rather have a clean shirt?" Mark was somewhat surprised at her request.

"No, I want to keep your scent from the shirt you were yesterday as a reminder to me whenever we are apart from each other," Chris explained

"Do you mean this shirt? Here you go." Mark complied and took out the shirt he wore the day before from his luggage. He added, "I hope to be with you at all times, not needing any reminder of the woman I just spent the most glorious week in my life.

The ferry ride back to Seattle saddened both Mark and Chris as they watched Crystal Cove disappear from the distance. It was early evening when they arrived at their apartment complex. They each went to their respective apartment to drop off their personal belongings; sort through their mail, check phone messages, unpacked and Mark wanted to take a shower before getting together. They planned to meet at her apartment for dinner. When Mark came upstairs, he saw Chris standing by the kitchen sink just looking out the window, seemingly at peace and in deep thoughts. Mark came from behind to wrap his arms around her waist and whispered, "I hope you were thinking about me in that dreamy look you had just a moment ago."

Chris responded, "Would you like to know what I was thinking, but if you must know, yes, I was imagining us living in that blue house. I know it is only a dream, which by the way, it is still free to dream. I did not have much food in the house, but I found a frozen pizza, which is in the oven now. There are a couple of bottles of wine in the fridge, but I will have root beer instead."

"I think I will have the same thing. After all those decadent meals, we had at Crystal Cove, pizza and root beer sound refreshing. Do you happen to have any chilled mugs? If not, how would you like your root beer served, over ice, with vanilla ice cream, or just in the bottle? I have plenty of vanilla ice cream in my freezer. I will get it. You know I am not into dessert, but ice cream must have at all times." Mark stated before going downstairs.

They enjoyed their simple dinner of pizza and root beer in her kitchen table. Mark could not thank Chris enough for inviting him to Crystal Cove. She continued to talk about the blue house and the changes she would make to put in her signature. Mark reached for her hand and kissed it. Before things get started, she had to say something to Mark.

"Mark, how much do you know about what happens to women once a month?" asked Chris.

"Do you mean about having a period once a month? I just know it happens to women. That is about the extent of my knowledge on that subject. What brought that on, if I may ask?" asked Mark.

"Well, yes, that is what I am talking about. Mine came today. For me, the process will last anywhere from three to five days, while others last longer than that. Let me warn you on what happens to me during those days so that you would not think I am crazy. I can be moody, sensitive to touch or have my feelings hurt easily, cry for no reason, cramps in my stomach area, and not wanting intimacy. You can hold me and cuddle me. Some women can get violent, not me. Are you glad it is only temporary?" Chris wanted to let Mark know.

"Thank you for telling me. I would never think of you as being crazy. Still, I want to stay with you tonight and just cuddle. I love snuggling with you that is if it is okay. I will go if you want me to go home." Mark sounded sympathetic

Mark and Chris continued their relationship and maintained separate residency. He would come up during the middle of the night and stay until wee hours of the morning.

Days and weeks continued to roll as their love grew stronger. Chris started her new job and worked long hours. Mark went on a couple of business trips shortly after their return from Crystal Cove Island, each trip lasting four to five days. Their work schedule kept them apart most of the time leading up to the primary holidays. They managed to spend quality time together during Thanksgiving and Christmas, with their friends at the apartment complex. When Worldwide Aeronautics gave their employees one week furlough during the end of the year, Chris and Mark spent New Years at Crystal Cove Island. Unknowingly, it would be their last vacation together at Crystal Cove Inn. The U.S. Government sent Mark on business trips more frequent, longer duration, which the separation became harder and harder for both of them. Regardless of where Mark might be, he never missed the phone calls to Chris, even just to hear her voice. After a week on another trip, Mark surprised Chris by being home unexpectedly. Although Chris kept herself busy at work, she was so happy to see him at home. She could not control her excitement the moment she saw Mark sitting in her living room. She ran to Mark and sat on his lap smothering him with kisses. He kissed her back, but his kisses were not the same. She sensed he had a lot on his mind, preoccupied and somewhat strained.

"What is the matter, Mark? Are you not happy to see me?" Chris asked Mark, with a great deal of concern.

"You are the only sane thing in my life. I love you more than my life. I want you to know that. I have missed you so much; it hurts. There are many things I must tell you in such a short time, so listen my love carefully. After I leave you here today, I will be on a special assignment requiring me to be in and out of the country for about a year. I just got the assignment this morning. For your protection, I am sorry I cannot tell you any more details as to where I will be or let you know when I will be home. I need you to trust me on this." It was difficult for Mark to ask her to wait for him and not be able to provide any explanation or more information.

Chris could not understand what he was saying; tears started to fall while listening to Mark's instructions. Deep in her heart, she knew this was likely to happen, still, how does one prepare for this situation?

"When will I be able to see you again? What do you mean about "in and out?" Are you in any danger? I love you." Chris did not like the responses from Mark.

"I love you more than you will ever know. I am sorry, I cannot explain a lot to you, my love. I need you to be brave and stay strong, as I know you can. After I leave, you will not be able to contact me like the way we have done, but I will get in touch with you when I can. It will only be for a year. I need you to promise me that you will wait for me. Things will look unusual for the next couple of days, but do not be alarmed and try to stay calm. It is important that you denounce knowing anything about me. I know I am asking a lot from you, but you have to trust me. I promise I will come back to you after this job is over. Remember, you did not know me, other than being my neighbor, regardless of how much people will try to get information from you. I placed a small blue luggage in your closet. Do not part with this luggage until we are together again. Someone will call you with the code word of "crystal-cove." That is when you can open the luggage. Until we see each other again, please keep the faith and trust in our love. Continue loving me as I love you. I have to leave now." Mark held her for a long time. He kissed her passionately before walking out the door.

CHAPTER 10

THE DOUBLE LIFE

The following morning, there were commotions downstairs in Mark's apartment, as if someone was desperately trying to get in. After a few minutes, the noise stopped. Then, some people were talking by the stairway. The apartment manager was downstairs, opening Mark's door with three men around him. They walked up to Chris's apartment looking for Mark.

"Good morning, Chris. Sorry, to bother you, but some government authorities are looking for Mark." The apartment manager said.

"Good morning, ma'am. We are from the U.S. Government, looking for Mark Ingram. Have you seen him lately? We just want to ask him some questions." One of the agents inquired.

"I ran into him at the parking lot on Tuesday morning when I went to work. I heard his TV on the following night. He pretty much kept to himself, except when there is an event at the clubhouse. May I ask why you are looking for him? What seems to be the problem? Do you have any business card, in the event I see or hear from him?" Chris politely asked.

"No, ma'am, we just want to talk to him. Thank you for your time. May we call on you again? Do not hesitate to call us, when you see him around. Do not approach him without us. "Officer #2 stated.

"Oh, sure, just let me know how I can help. Do you have a business card?" Chris asked the other agent.

When the officers left, Chris wondered about Mark, but she remembered that she promised to trust Mark. From the beginning, he has been a Godsend to her. How could she possibly question Mark's integrity?

Mark has been gone less than a month, not a word or a phone call from him. Nevertheless, Chris misses Mark every day that passes. She has been unable to sleep at night, seemingly tired most of the time; sometimes she cannot keep her food down or occasionally feeling dizzy. Still, she continued her rigorous schedule and ate lightly, mostly salads, fruits and vegetables and drinking lots of fluids. Her conditioned seemed to have improved and kept herself busy with work. During those quiet times when she is at home, she finds herself sitting by the phone, hoping to hear Mark's voice on the other end. At times she merely stares out her front window imagining him walking in through the gate entrance, waving at her with a big smile on his face. She had envisioned this picture in her mind that gives her some comfort and to think happy thoughts of Mark.

The winter snow in Everett, Washington started to melt, creating mini waterfalls streaming down along the hillsides, in addition to the spring flowers of iris, tulips, and hostas began peeking through the snow-covered ground, signs that spring weather brings new life and blossoming months that bring meaningful growth and rejuvenation in its wake. Moreover, as the spring season is undoubtedly in the forecast, it is a welcoming reminder that a major project that Chris has been working on long and hard would be coming to fruition. This achievement would serve as her crowning glory both professionally and personally.

World-Wide Aeronautics Company would become a model company to be first aeronautics company to convert towards a 'paperless environment' to an online data in support of the environ meal programs to 'save the trees' in the Northern Pacific Coast region. With the collaboration and support from the State of Washington, World-Wide Aeronautics would significantly reduce their day-to-day operating cost, reduction in business tax, just to name a couple of enormous cost benefits and most of all contributing to 'Saving the Planet' initiative supported by the EPA (Environmental Protection Agency)

Upon completion of the online conversion for World-Wide

Aeronautics Co, Chris received well-deserved accolades from the upper management as well as from her team. Under her flawless leadership and her group consisting of thirty-six employees delivered the much-publicized project under budget and two weeks ahead of a nearly impossible deadline. Many skeptics who were mostly stockholders and the elite company officers could not believe that a newly promoted Director, who was only twenty-eight years old, could deliver such a challenging project. Silently, Chris admittedly that Mark had been right from the very beginning when he made the statement that age does not define you. More importantly, believing in yourself, having that confidence and listening to your heart will get you through bad times as well as good times. At that moment, tears just stream down her face, because the one person that pulled her through was Mark.

Chris received a message from the secretary of the company CEO instructing her to attend a meeting on Tuesday at 10:00 AM. Not knowing anything about the meeting. Chris felt somewhat nervous as to why she was being summoned to attend. The day of the meeting the secretary took her to a conference room where the people in the room applauded as she walked in. The only person she knew in the place was her ex-boss who flew in from South Carolina for this special occasion. She recognized the people in the place by their picture in the company magazine given to the employees of World-Wide Aeronautics. The CEO introduced her to all the elite management team who all came up to her to congratulate her on her accomplishment. She was presented with an envelope which contained a check for fifty-thousand dollars. Tears started to stream down her face. The CEO standing next to her hugged her and thanked her for a job well done. She wanted to excuse herself to share her good fortune with her team. They asked her to wait because her entire team will each be given a check for ten-thousand dollars. Chris could not be more joyous and excited about her team. In her excitement, she remembered hugging each one of them and saying thank you on behalf of the entire team.

By the time she got back to her department, most of them just got back from lunch. Chris has been very popular, well respected by her colleagues and well-liked by her employees. Some noticed that she had been crying. They all knew that she had been summoned to the CEO office. Chris had been gone a long time. They wondered what could have happened at the meeting. One of the team leads approached Chris to ask her about having a pot-luck luncheon in the office to celebrate the completion of the project. Chris suggested that instead of a pot-luck, she would have a catered lunch in celebration of their team's accomplishment. She gave them all a big smile.

Chris planned the catered luncheon that Friday. While they ate their lunch, Chris was holding a bunch of envelopes in her hand. Some speculated that the envelope contained a gift certificate. She made a couple of announcements in behalf of the upp0er management, thanking them all for their hard work and long hours. She added giving a half the crew a half a day off after lunch or on a different day. Everyone cheered on the announcements, but they were anxious about the envelopes Chris has in her hands. Then, she said that she would be passing out an envelope to each member of the team, a gift from the upper management. All she asked was to wait until all of them were distributed before opening. As soon as they opened their envelope, some cried, some screamed with excitement, and some could not believe the check of ten-thousand dollars they each received. They each came up to Chris and hugged her. They formed a big circle for the group hug. The whole office celebrated, almost no one wanted to leave the room. What a sight to see.

Chris continued to keep herself busy by working long hours to avoid being home without Mark. Sometimes her ex-boss would ask for some assistance, needing her to travel to South Carolina. Working long hours and traveling may have caught up with her. She has been unable to shake off the 'flu-like-bug' that seems to continue to linger. To take the edge out of whatever ailment or flu bug she may have contracted along the way, she poured herself a glass of wine hoping to make her feel better. After she finished half the glass of wine, she was feeling sleepy, so she lay on the floor in front of the fireplace, remembering the time with Mark at the Crystal Cove Inn. As she closed her eyes and started dreaming about Mark making love to her, it felt as though his scent and the feel of his body moving along with her body lingered until wee hours of the night. The oddest part of the dream was when she felt Mark carrying her to the bedroom. After he kissed her passionately as he laid her down, he seemed to have disappeared. She woke up in her bed, not knowing how she got there, so she called out to Mark, no answer. The dream felt so real; maybe Mark might be in the kitchen reading the paper. She got up right away to look all around the apartment, and nothing seems to be out of place. The only thing she noticed was the unsecured chain on the door. She must have forgotten to put the chain up last night. Still thinking about the dream that she kept playing in her mind, it put a smile on her face as she went to work happily. When she got home, she still was not feeling 100%, so she took a nap on the couch. There was a knock at the door, and it woke her up. Since the incident with Larry, she got in the habit of looking through the peephole before opening the door. It was Sandy.

"Hey, what brings you here? How are you?" Chris asked.

"Sorry, did I wake you up?" Sandy felt terrible that she awakened Chris from a nap.

"It's okay; it was time for me to get up anyway and fix my dinner. Have you had your dinner yet? Can I offer you coffee or tea? I was just about to have a sandwich. Would you like one?" Chris asked.

"Okay, if it is not too much. I will put on the teakettle." Sandy replied.

"What do you think happened to Mark? He just vanished. For as long as he lived downstairs, I did not see anyone come to visit him. He was always polite and very caring during the Larry incident. Have you heard any more news on Mark?" Chris inquired.

"The apartment manager talked to the authorities about Mark. Those so-called "government" people were not who they claimed to be. When the manager tried to get in touch with them, the phone numbers had been disconnected and no forwarding numbers. Someone paid for Mark's lease and took all his belongings. They claimed to be a relative of Mark's, not from the government. The manager speculated that Mark was a spy or some covert agent on a mission. He thinks Mark had to be a good guy, but his enemies may have uncovered his identity. Consequently, he vanished." according to Sandy

"He did tell me once he worked for the government. He said his job was boring, so he did not talk about it. You were probably the closest person to him. What did you find out about him?" Chris was playing the part of not knowing much about Mark.

"I liked him. He had all the qualities of a man you would want to have as a partner. I tried to get to know him, but there was that sense of politeness he does not want to hurt your feelings. He is kind and knew how to treat a woman. I think he has someone very special but may not know how lucky she is, whoever she might be. We became just good friends." Sandy shared how she felt about Mark, which she has never shared with anyone before.

"He was such a good neighbor, very protective especially during the incident with Larry. Thank goodness, he is in jail." Chris concurred

"I better get going. It was nice chatting with you and thank you for the meal. We need to get together soon, even if it is just going to the movies. Lorraine has been busy with Pete since he got back. He is a good man, like Mark. Good night, Chris." Sandy went back to her apartment.

Sandy and Chris became close friends since that time. The "circle of friends," Sandy, Tom & Marie, Lorraine & Pete, remained loyal friends to one another. They got together for dinner at each other's apartment at least once a month. Occasionally, Mark's name would come up in the conversation. They wondered what might have happened to him. He just seemed to have disappeared. There were some talks about Mark being a spy or a secret agent on some detail work. Chris just went along with the conversation, not offering any information to the kind of work he was doing. She continued to maintain her innocence as she promised Mark. All she knew was that she was missing him a lot. There were times when Chris would stop for a moment at the bottom of the stairs, hoping to see Mark walk out of his apartment. Mark's apartment has been empty for a while.

One Saturday morning, Chris happened to be in the middle of fixing breakfast. The tea kettle just started to whistle when the phone rang. She got all excited hoping that Mark would be on the other end of the line.

"Hello..." Chris answered.

"Is this Christina Jensen?" The person asked.

"Yes, it is. Who is this?" Chris asked. She did not recognize the voice.

"Crystal Cove" replied, and then, the dial tone

Chris did not know what to make of the call, but she remembered Mark's instructions about the blue luggage. She went to retrieve the luggage and brought it out on the bed to open the luggage. The luggage contained lots of papers, documents, and a ring box. On the very top of the documents, she found an envelope with her name on it. It read...

"My darling, Chris, the love of my life, if you are reading this letter, please know that I am all right and missing you each day we are not together. I am sorry to have put you through a lot and ask you to continue to be strong awhile longer and to believe in our love that will sustain us until we are together again. I know it is unfair for me to ask you to wait for me for a year. However, if you find that special man that makes you very happy, I am releasing you from any promises you made to me. I want you to be happy and wish you the best. The short time we spent together had been the happiest time in my life. You have my heart and soul. Not being with you makes each hour seems like a day. If by chance, we get through this year, I promise that I will make good on the paper we signed at that small chapel by asking you to marry me. As a down payment on my promise, you will find other documents that support my intentions. My love, the blue house you loved so much, the deed, title and the keys are yours. Yes, you own the house fully and additional cash to furnish the house to your heart's content. Do you remember the morning you woke up and found a note next to your pillow? I went to a realtor to put a down payment on the blue house. Now, it is yours. This will be our home to raise our family and grow old together. I can almost see the happiness in your face. Lastly, please accept my ring as a token of my never-ending love for you. The moment I saw this ring, I saw you immediately, beautiful, brilliant, has the clarity of pure rainwater and most of all, one of a kind. For now, my love, think happy thoughts. I LOVE YOU...Mark.

After reading the letter from Mark, she could not feel any lonelier than she felt, not having Mark there to share the happiness of receiving such gifts. It would be meaningless not being able to share this with the man she loves. If the price to pay to receive such gifts meant separating from Mark, she would give it all back just to have Mark by her side. Tears flowed at the thought of not seeing him again. She cried herself to sleep. Chris needed to keep the faith and continue trusting Mark's word. She cannot make sudden changes, for the sake of keeping him safe.

CHAPTER 11

Trip to the Blue House

Work kept Chris busy, but there was never a day that she did not think of Mark. Still, she cannot shake the "flu bug" that has been lingering since Mark left. Perhaps, she needed to get away for the weekend to try to get better. The first thing that came to her mind was Crystal Cove, where she feels the closest to Mark. She took the 3:00 o'clock afternoon ferry. When she arrived at Crystal Cove Island, she rented a golf cart and went directly to the blue house. As she approached the house, happy memories flashed before her eyes as she walked through the house. It put a smile on her face knowing they own this lovely house. To her delight, the key opened the front door, and the electricity appeared to be working. She picked up the wall phone in the kitchen and got a dial tone. In the living room, a cozy rocking chair with a lap blanket well placed in front of the wood-burning fireplace that dominated the entire wall. On one side of the fireplace, a neatly stacked of firewood in the woodbin and on the other side a brand new set of fireplace accessories completed the room. In the center of the fireplace an old-fashioned wood-burning stove that adds a final touch to country living. Past the living room, cute dining room/kitchen has a table with four chairs and modern appliances, for a gourmet cook. The cabinets and drawers contained dishes, glasses, and silver wares. Near the stove/oven was a newly added workbench, which will be handy to pre-stage hot dishes before placing them on the table. What caught her eye was this small wooden box with her name carved on top of the box. When she opened it, it was full of her favorite tea bags. On the stovetop, a whistling tea kettle awaits. Seeing all of this, it put a big smile on her face, knowing that all the details in this house have Mark's signature on every one of them. She quietly said to herself, "Mark, I am home. I love you."

To complete the tour, she proceeded to check out the rest of the house. A hallway leads to the bedrooms. On the right side, two small bedrooms with adjoining bathroom and on the left the bigger bedroom have a queen size bed with its own bathroom. Chris went back to the kitchen to brew some tea. Symbolically, she brought out two teacups to commemorate this event. She poured tea into both cups, then, she lightly tapped the cup and said, "Here is to you, Mark. I wish you were here with me." She brought her cup of tea in the living room and sat on the rocking chair by the fireplace. Chris threw in a couple of logs in the wood stove to warm up the house. She heard a knock at the door, not expecting anyone; she remained quiet and ignored the knocking. The knocking persisted, she decided to peek out the window and saw a woman standing there.

"Hello, may I help you?" Chris asked.

The woman answered, "Yes, you may. I need directions …

"I am sorry, but your voice sounds so familiar to me." Chris interrupted the woman and added, "It cannot be…Mark?"

"Yes, it is me," Mark said. "Do not make any sudden moves towards me. I am sorry for the disguise, but we have to be careful and pretend we are just strangers, giving me directions. I just wanted to see you and let you know that I am here, not far from you. Come out to the porch and start pointing as if you are giving me directions. Try not to stare at me." Mark requested.

In her excitement, she almost dropped her cup of tea. Chris complied, "I have missed you so much. I do not want you to go. I want to kiss you."

"I will be coming back tonight, so leave the back door unlocked," Mark told her to wait a few more hours. "Sorry, for the "dress-up," but I needed an innocent disguise to see you. We have to be very cautious from here on, even in this place. I will see you soon my love. I love you. Now, wave to me and put on a happy smile."

Chris could not be happier knowing she will be seeing Mark in a few hours. She drove the golf cart to a neighborhood grocery store to get some snacks and a bottle of wine to celebrate his homecoming. Near the cashier's stand, there were bunches of lavender flowers, so she picked up a bunch. Still, not feeling well, she managed to fix some sandwiches to go with the wine. While waiting for Mark, she had a half a glass of wine, hoping she would feel better. Mark quietly entered the back door to find Chris asleep in the rocking chair. He knelt down by her side and saw the ring on her finger. He just watched her lovingly for a minute before he scooped her from the rocking chair and carried her to the bedroom. She woke up and put her arms around his neck to kiss him all over his face until she passionately kisses him.

"I am so happy you are here with me. We have a lot to talk about." She said with excitement in her voice.

"Sssshhh, I am happy to be back, my love." He laid her down and started to undress her. "You know how I want to sleep with you, skin to skin only. Your skin is so soft and silky, just as I remembered it to be. I love you so much."

They made love all night, making up for some lost time. They had so much to catch up on, but it was nearly dawn, Mark told her, "I have to leave soon. I will try to come back tonight if it is safe."

"You promise," she said

Mark quickly replied, "Please remain patient awhile longer until we can be together. I know you have to go back on Sunday, but know I am never far from you. I love you with all my heart." He reminded her to be safe, take good care and be careful not to make too many changes to her routine. He hugged and kissed her for a long time, then left using the back door.

Chris got up to make some tea. She could not go back to sleep, so she watched the sunrise. It was as spectacular as the sunset. Mornings are especially difficult for Chris. She seemed to be dizzy and nauseous at the same time. Something dawned on her, with all the things happening around her, she missed her period last month, and after seeing Mark, she should have had her period this month. That would be two months of misses. Could this be what she thinks? There was a bit of excitement at the thought of the possibility of being pregnant with Mark's child.

If he comes back tonight, she is not sure if she should even mention the prospect of being a father. How will he take it? Maybe, she should wait until she is sure. Mark came back that night as he promised but in a different disguise.

They held on to each other and made love, not knowing when they will see each other again. The dawn started to break when Mark began to explain that he could not talk about his mission but told her to be patient until he returns. The little she knows about his work, the safer it would be for both of them.

"Mark, are you in any kind of danger?" asked Chris

Mark reassured her by telling her. "There is always an element of danger on any kind of work." He said it so that she would not worry too much. In a kidding way, Mark said, "If something were to happen to me, you would be a very wealthy woman and young enough to find a new partner. Don't worry; I will be back as I promised."

Chris did not care for that statement and said, "that statement does not amuse me. It is not the right thing to say. I will hold you to your promise, to come back to me even if it takes a lifetime."

Mark sensed it touched a sensitive nerve that offended Chris. He looked at her in the eye and said, "I am sorry. I will not do that again. Let us change the subject, shall we? The ring looks beautiful on your finger." he commented

"Oh, so you noticed. It is simply exquisite and timeless piece of jewelry I will ever own. More importantly, I love the ring because of what it represents, the love and sincerity from a man who gave it to me. I love you, Mark."

"Does it mean you accept my proposal to marry me?" Mark implored

Chris replied. "A thousand yesses, I will marry you."

"Chris, you made me a very happy man. I love you very much. I cannot wait for this job to be completed so that we can be together, live in this house, raise our family and grow old together." Mark said with a smile on his face.

"Would you like to have children right away? How many kids did you have in mind?" Chris asked with a great deal of interest and excitement.

"Ideally, having one of each would be perfect, especially if our daughter looks as beautiful as her mommy. It will be a tough battle when she starts dating. We better set the rules; one would be no dating until the age of thirty. Would you agree?" Mark meant well if it was a reasonable rule Chris might have agreed.

"We may be getting ahead of ourselves. Really, at age thirty. Do you not think it is rather harsh? Falling in love happens when your heart and mind come together to make it right, just like the way I fell in love with you. There is no age requirement when it comes to falling in love, but I love listening how protective you will be with your daughter. "Chris explained her take on the matter.

"You are right. There is no time requirement when it comes to falling in love. It just happens, I know." Mark agreed with Chris. He went on to say, "I am glad you are on my team –– a winning team."

"Just as falling in love has no time requirement, babies have a way of coming into this world unexpectedly," Chris commented to see his reaction.

With the look of surprise, Mark quickly asked, "Are you trying to tell me something? Why did you mention babies?"

"No reason, the word just came out. I was not going to mention it until I knew for sure, but I have had two missed periods, and I have not been feeling well. With what was happening to you and the long hours at work, it could be that it has finally caught up with me. I made an appointment to see my doctor when I get back, but I just had to come to Crystal Cove because I missed you so much I wanted to feel you near me. Seeing you and having this time together made me feel so much better." Chris had mixed emotions of sadness knowing that Mark will be leaving in a few hours. Chris went on to say, "Oh, Mark, I hope to have a part of you growing inside of me."

"Chris that would be the best gift you could give me, to be a father to our child. However, it would mean having you to take care of our child by yourself until my contract is complete. I hope and pray that I will be back before our child arrives." Mark felt happy at the thought of being a father but had some concern he would not be around most of the time.

Chris responded, "There are lots of single mothers raising their children by themselves. I have a great job with excellent medical benefits, should not be a problem."

"You know I do not mean that. I want to feel the first kick, hearing the heartbeat, watching your cute belly grow, and be present when he or she arrives into this world. Most of all, I want to be there for you." Mark's eyes were welling up as he was making his statement.

"Oh, Mark, that means a lot to me for you to say that." Chris hugged Mark as she said it. "I also want you to be there every step of the process. However, we may be getting ahead of ourselves. It could be a false alarm. If so, not to worry, we will not start without you." she went on to say.

"I will be leaving soon, my love. I love you and please, take good care of yourself until I see you again." Mark pleaded. Chris could not hold her tears, so he pulled her towards him and held her for a long time. He kissed her before walking out the back door.

Before leaving the house, Chris double-checked the windows and doors were closed and in a lock position. She rechecked the fireplace, to make sure there were no embers left. Mark did the same thing earlier, putting the wood neatly in the woodbin, cups, and dishes back in the cupboards, and emptied trash cans. Mark's attention to details secured the house before he left. Chris took the noon ferry back to Seattle. When she got home, there were a couple of messages from her friends in the apartment complex, wanting to know where she was. She called them back to let them know that she went away for the weekend. Next time, she promised to let them know whenever she was going out of town. It makes sense; she did not want to alarm them and bring attention to herself.

Monday morning, Chris went to work as usual. Since HR department was located next door to the Health Facilities department, she decided to schedule a mini tour of their facilities, as an HR Admin representative. World-Wide Aeronautics Company, who employs hundreds of engineers, mechanics, assemblymen/women, etc., they have a mini-hospital in the event of emergencies. Staff with a resident doctor, a nurse and an EMT (emergency management team) as first responders on the job injuries, as a company they have received awards for excellence. Also, the company has a helicopter available seven days a week, twenty-four hours a day to transport severe injuries to nearby trauma hospitals. They even have counselors to handle, drug addictions, mental health issues and other addictions. After the tour, Chris was amazed and proud of World-Wide Aeronautics Company to have such health services for their employees. However, even with all the modern, sophisticated facilities, World-Wide Aeronautics Company does not have the "service" she needs for her ailment.

CHAPTER 12

THE GIFT FROM GOD

Chris contacted her doctor to make an appointment for an annual physical. She went to see Dr. Sara McQueen.

"Good morning, Chris. How are you? Dr. McQueen greeted Chris

"Hello, Dr. McQueen. I haven't been feeling well lately." Chris admitted

"According to our records, it has been a couple of years since your last physical. You are overdue for one. Is there something else that brings you in to see me?" Dr. McQueen asked

"I am not sure, but I think I may be pregnant. At first, I thought traveling on business trips and working long hours may have caught up with me. However, I have missed my period two months in a row and feeling nauseous and dizzy mostly in the morning. "Chris sheepishly admitted.

"Okay, I will order additional tests, and we should get the results right away while we do your physical exam." Dr. McQueen replied

Chris asked, "Doctor if I am not pregnant I would like to discuss the different types of preventions other than the pill." Chris asked

"Let us get started. First, I will need to ask you for a urine sample, then; we will complete your physical. The lab results will not be known for a couple of days. However, we will know more when your urine test comes back in a few minutes. Dr. McQueen completed the exam and told Chris to get dressed. Come to the office to discuss the result of the urine tests. They waited for the nurse to bring in the results. The doctor told her the preliminary test results, "Well, Chris, your pregnancy test came back positive, which you already suspected. All your vital signs are excellent. The lab work will not be available for a couple of days or so. I will call you for the follow-up appointments once I get all the results. Dr. McQueen noticed a smile and a sense of relief on Chris' face, "so, I take it that you are happy with the pregnancy result?"

Chris quickly replied, "Is it that obvious? Thank you, Dr. McQueen."

Several days passed when Chris received a message from Dr. McQueen's office. The doctor's office just closed, so she decided to take the following morning off to return the call, "Hello, Dr. McQueen. It is Chris Jensen returning your call."

Dr. McQueen responded, "Hi Chris, let me pull up your records. Your blood results came back "normal" across the board. You are definitely pregnant, eight to ten weeks along. Therefore, you are looking at having your baby around the early part in September. Congratulations!" Dr. McQueen added, "You will now be seeing an OB/GYN. I would recommend Dr. Paul Rogers unless you have someone in mind. My nurse can make the follow-up appointment with Dr. Rogers in a week or so. In the meantime, have many saltine crackers handy for the nausea, eat wisely for two, try not to work long hours, and just take good care of yourself. Don't hesitate to call me, if you have questions or concerns." Dr. McQueen suggested

"Thank you, doctor." Chris remained quiet while the doctor was giving her advice. She felt her belly knowing that a part of Mark was growing inside of her. Oh, how she wanted Mark to have been there at that moment, tears started to stream down her face. There was enough time to do a quick run before going in the office. In her route, she passed the bus stop where she and Mark waited for the rain to stop. At that moment, she stood on the back of the bench, running her fingers on the bench where Mark would have sat as he held her close. Tears were streaming down her face as she tried to hug the bench. There was another person who just got there to wait for the bus. She composed herself and sat up as she wiped the tears from her face. She stood up to continue her run when the person grabbed her arm and said, "Chris, it is Mark. Do not make any sudden moves towards me. Walk towards the alley and wait for me."

Chris complied and waited in the alley for Mark. As he came around the corner, he grabbed her to hug and kiss her. "I followed you from the apartment. Are you all right?" Mark asked

"Mark, Mark, I cannot do this anymore." cried Chris

"Sssshhh, yes, you can. I am holding you right now. As I said, I am never far from you. I can tell when you need me, like right now. I saw that you have not gone to work and you are out here; something was not right." Mark was concerned

"I just found out that we are going to have a baby sometime in September. I did not know when I was going to see you to tell you our good news. Oh, Mark, I miss you every day we are not together." Chris hugged Mark even tighter.

"I know, baby, just hold on a while longer for the sake of our baby. I am so happy and looking forward to our future together, raising our family. I will come to you whenever I can. I should be back before our baby is born, but record, make notes and jot down whatever information about our baby as if I was with you every step of the way. Be brave; take good care of yourself and our baby. The bus is coming I will have to go. I love you my darling." Mark sincerely meant every word. "Here comes the bus. I am going to walk you home part of the way, then, I will walk away. Kiss me before the bus gets here."

"When will I see you again?" Chris asked

"I will be keeping an eye on you to watch your belly get bigger with our baby. Keeping you and the baby in my thoughts at all times will sustain me the rest of the time. Keep happy thoughts and the faith that I will be back. This is where I leave you. Will you be all right, sweetheart?" Take care and stay safe. I love you…" Mark winked at her.

The spring weather brings many types of pollen in the air, allergy season in full bloom causing sneezing and wheezing. Mark was able to see Chris in the apartment three more times, Easter, Memorial Day and 4th of July. The months rolled by, but not fast enough for Chris, who was in her fifth month of pregnancy and was starting to show. She could not hide the bulge she had been hiding for months. Naturally, curious seekers were shy to ask, so she decided to let others know about her pregnancy, starting with her circle of friends. She invited them all to dinner at her place. They have not seen her for several months. They were surprised to see her with a bulge but held back their curiosity until they heard from Chris. After dinner, she told them a story about having an affair in South Carolina that resulted in her pregnancy. They asked questions, and she made up the answers as she went along. The hardest question they asked was why she decided to keep the baby if it was just an affair. Trying to give them the straight answer was difficult, but she had to keep the story going. Her main reason for keeping the baby was due to her religious beliefs against abortion. They commended her for making the choice and accepting the responsibilities of having a child. Financially, they knew Chris has a good job, with significant medical benefits. They all offered their support and volunteered to help her with babysitting duty. That was a big load off her mind by telling her second family. Having told her friends, it became easier to tell her co-workers the same story. They, too, understood her choices and were supportive of how courageous she will be as a single parent. However, she was growing weary that she has not seen Mark or heard from him since 4th of July weekend. She has no means of calling him.

During her last trimester, her coworkers and World-Wide Aeronautics Company management threw her a big baby shower. Not knowing the sex of the baby, she received many gift certificates at various stores. Chris was very popular with her subordinates and loyal to the upper management. The top management gave her a check for thirty-thousand dollars. It was not something that World-Wide Aeronautics Company often gives away, but they were so pleased with the project she worked on that was near impossible to deliver on time, yet, with her leadership, the project was completed two weeks before it was due and under the projected budget. The upper management thought very highly of her; they showed how valuable she was to the company. Of course, top management asked her not to disclose what she received. Nonetheless, she was extremely grateful for the check, which guarantees the baby's college fund. Most of her co-workers asked what her plans were after having the baby.

Chris answered, "I would like to take about 3 or 4 months to bond with my baby before coming back to work. As a single mother, I will need a job to sustain us, besides I will miss working here. You have been so good to me during the conversion project that won us several awards, and I truly value your genuine support for my choices that meant a lot to me. Thank you all so much for your generous gifts that my baby and I will put it to good use. With that said, we have a lot of work, so let us get back to it before I get sentimental."

Labor Day weekend meant the traditional BBQ at the clubhouse with her circle of friends and about twenty families joining in the celebration. It also meant Chris' due date to have the baby. At the picnic, the apartment management provided the hamburgers and hot dogs, while the families provided the potluck style dishes. The men cooked the burgers and hot dogs. The women arranged the table and the potluck dishes. The weather condition could not have been any better, clear skies, sunny and warm. Everyone was enjoying the food, games, or just catching up with their neighbors. The apartment manager came to the gathering to announce some upcoming improvements to the apartment complex. Detailed information on the improvements affecting the tenants is on the bulletin board near the manager's office. Just about, everyone cheered and clapped in support of the significant improvements planned. As a final announcement, the manager said, "On the sad note, some of you may remember a former tenant by the name of Mark Ingram. It was announced on the local news station that keeps track of local men and women who become casualties of war, announced that Mark Ingram from Everett, Washington was one of the three men from Special Forces that was killed in action in the Middle East."

When Chris heard Mark's name, Chris felt light-headed and fainted. They called 911 immediately, and the ambulance took her to ER right away. The tending physician happened to be Dr. Spencer, who notified Chris's OB/GYN that she was admitted to the ER for exhaustion.

"Hello, Chris, we have notified Dr. Rodgers that you have been admitted to the ER. He is on his way in to examine you to make sure you and the baby are just fine. Your due date is nearing. Are you feeling all right?" asked Dr. Spencer

"Yes, doctor. I felt a little light headed earlier." Chris explained

Dr. Rodgers gave her an exam and told her to stay in the hospital overnight for observation. Her circle of friends from the apartment followed her to the hospital and waited until they got the word that she is in stable condition, but will have to be kept overnight for observations. They have given her a mild sedation so that she will be asleep most of the night. The nurse advised them to go home and come back in the morning. Since Tom recently retired after twenty-five years as a principal and Marie was a volunteer worker, they went to the hospital the following morning. They went directly to Chris' room and saw that a couple of doctors were there, talking to Chris. She acknowledged Tom and Marie by giving them a small wave. They brought a bouquet of flowers to cheer her up. The doctors completed their exam and left the room. It was just the three of them in the room.

Tom hugged Chris and shared his sadness, "I am sorry to hear about Mark. I know he was a good neighbor to you. At one point, Marie and I thought that you two had something going. Mark would tell us how he felt about you. He meant every word of it. We were not sure if you knew how much he really wanted you."

Marie added, "When it was just the three of us, he would admit to us his feelings towards you. Did you know how he felt about you?

Chris admitted, "Yes, I did. I have wanted to tell you the truth about Mark and me early on. We have been together ever since I got my promotion. However, because of his line of work, we had to be discreet. Whenever Mark came to see me, he would be in disguise, unspecified location, rarely at the apartment. A couple of days before they raided his apartment, Mark told me to denounce him. He has always been so mysterious about what he did for work. I kept asking until he told me that it was best for all of us to denounce Mark. Now, that he is gone, it doesn't matter anymore."

Tom asked, "Did you have a way of contacting him?"

"No, Mark always came to me unexpectedly, only to stay for a few hours. The last time I saw him was 4th of July weekend." Chris went on to say, "By the way, this baby I am carrying is Mark's. Fortunately, he knew I was carrying his child. He promised he would be here when the baby arrives. Now, he will not be able to keep his promise.

Tom had to say it, "Chris, one thing I knew for sure about Mark, he was a man of his word. I am certain he would have kept his promise."

"Thank you for saying that. Now, that he is gone, I don't know how to go on without him." Chris said

"Chris, you must not forget, you have a baby about to be born. He or she is part of Mark that will go on with you. You will need to find that strength and the will to be strong for you and your baby. Please know that you have us and others. Things may look dark right now, but you are an independent, responsible person that will be an excellent parent for your child." Marie stated her confidence in Chris.

"Just to ask, did Mark give you any information on whom or how to reach out in the event of something like this happened," Tom asked

"Mark always re-assured me, the less we knew about him, the safer we would all be, not to mention exposing the mission. He kept promising that he will be back and to trust him on this important matter," she said

Marie inquired, "What are you going to do after you have the baby?"

"I do not know. Mark bought us a house in Crystal Cove earlier this year, to raise our family. We have spent quality time there. I have to go back there to bond with my baby and to feel Mark around me even though he is gone. He must have planned all this, knowing this might happened. I would like you two to promise me that you will visit us as often as you can. I know you will love it on Crystal Cove Island just as we did." Chris was trying to convince Tom and Marie to move near her.

Tom replied, "Of course, now, that I am retired, we should have plenty of time to come and visit your paradise. We have never been there, but have seen lots of travel advertisement on the island. It is just in our backyard and a ferry ride from Seattle. Knowing that you will be living there with your little one, we will come for sure."

"Speaking of my little one, the doctors recommend bed rest until I have the baby, which is anytime now. The baby is in a position to come soon." You can hear a sense of excitement and anticipation from her voice. Chris went on to say, "I can feel Mark is watching over us."

Chris was in labor the following day. She asked Marie to videotape the moment her baby arrives into this world. The baby came into the world without any problems. "It is a boy." The doctor announced to everyone in the room. When Chris heard him cry, she, too, cried. They placed the baby on her chest so that the baby can hear a familiar heartbeat from mom. She called him Ben right away. She remembered Mark's brother name Benjamin that wished to have his name. After a few minutes "bonding" with the baby, the nurse took him to clean him up and take measurements, plus his footprints. Chris quietly said, "Thank you God for the blessing and Mark, wherever you are, your son Ben is here. I know you are watching over us. We love you."

They remained in the hospital for two more days. Tom and Marie came to pick them up and brought them to her apartment. When they got to the apartment complex, Chris stopped for a moment at the foot of the stairways, only a few steps from Mark's old apartment, to say, "Mark, your son is home." She had tears in her eyes as she was speaking. Marie offered to take the baby, so that she can walk up the stairs, with some assistance from Tom. The apartment had been prepared for a warm welcome for mom and son. In her bedroom, a baby bassinet was next to her bed. Marie volunteered to stay with her for a couple of days or until she gets her strength back. Lorraine and Pete flew up to see Chris and the baby.

Chris greeted Lorraine and Pete, "So happy to see you both. It is like old times. How do you like living in San Diego?"

"We are so happy there, surrounded by our families. You and the baby will have to come down and spend some time with us, you too, Sandy, Marie, and Tom." Lorraine was excited to see her friends again.

Tom and Marie were a big help to Chris. They cooked and shared meals with Chris. After a couple of weeks, her strength was back to normal and able to care for the baby on her own. The baby slept most of the night and a couple of long naps during the day. When the baby was awake, she would talk about his daddy Mark as if he was in the room. Even though Mark was gone, she can still imagine his presence as well as remembering his scent. She remembered Mark's shirt that she kept in her drawers and quickly took it out to wrap the baby with it. At night was when she missed Mark the most. She would close her eyes and imagine how Mark would be with his son. During the day, some of her neighbors would come by and visit or bring her food, so that she does not have to do much cooking since having the baby. After a month,

Chris thought long and hard about moving to Crystal Cove to her blue house. Although she would miss being with her second family in the apartment complex, she longed to start a life with her baby in the island where she and Mark talked about having a family and growing old together. Before turning in her 30-day notice to the apartment manager, she decided to share her plans with Tom, Marie, and Sandy. They were saddened to see her go, but they certainly understood her decision. She planned to move out at the end of October and be at Crystal Cove Island by November 1. Chris hired movers to move most of her things. The rest, she just gave away.

The last week of her stay in the apartment, she received an unexpected phone call from an insurance company representing Mark Ingram. They made an appointment to meet at Chris' apartment to go over some insurance benefits in which she was the designated beneficiary of his life insurance. The insurance company received the death certificate from the U.S. Government; the agent asked how she would like to receive the lump sum of money. The agent went on to ask for her financial advisor that would handle the transfer.

Chris stated, "I do not have my own personal agent, but I am with Fidelity Investment who currently has all my investments with World-Wide Aeronautics Company. I do have a card from Fidelity who contacted me previously to go over my portfolio. Here is his card.

"Would you mind if we talk to Fidelity together to go over this matter?" Insurance agent asked

The agent talked to the Fidelity agent to introduce himself and verified certain security matter to confirm and ensure e the identities of both agents. Chris was anxious to finish soon because the baby was just about due to be awake. They both were on the phone when the baby started to make some noises that required Chris to check on the baby.

"Ms. Jensen has to check on her baby, but we can go over a couple of details that does not require her presence, if that is okay with you?" the Harford agent stated

"It is fine with me, if Ms. Jensen is in agreement?" the Fidelity agent said. Chris nodded in agreement while she looks in on the baby.

"As I was saying, Ms. Jensen is a beneficiary of a life insurance, and we need to place the money where it would be advantageous to Ms. Jensen." Hartford agent said

"What amount of money are we talking about?" asked the Fidelity agent

"It is a rather large amount of money. The amount is two million dollars." Hartford agent said.

"Did I hear you right?" Fidelity agent asked

"Yes, I did say two million. " Hartford agent repeated

"Right now, we probably need to roll it into the money market fund, then, move it to an IRA. We would have to sit down with Ms. Jensen and go over the different options. For now, the interim option of putting it temporarily in IRA would avoid any luxury tax and penalty taxes that may be applicable. Let me give you her interim account number..." Fidelity agent said. He went on to say, "I will discuss with Ms. Jensen at a later time where she would like to invest her IRA account. Chris came back to the room with the baby.

"I got the account numbers, thank you. Let me just get Ms. Jensen's' signature, and I will wire transfer the check." Hartford agent stated

After talking to Fidelity, the Hartford agent turned to Chris, to let her know that she is receiving two million dollars from Mark's insurance. She looked shocked at the money she just received. Nonetheless, this was a high price to pay instead of Mark's life. She would rather have Mark than the money.

"Sorry, for not telling you the amount of money you just inherited. The check had your name and the full amount, which is a standard practice if you were to receive a smaller amount. Having Fidelity involved was safer and fewer fees involved. I could have just handed it to you and be on my way. If we did that, you would have had to pay so much taxes, luxury, inheritance, penalty, etc. By having it handled by your investor, Fidelity, you saved yourself about five-hundred thousand dollars of fees immediately. Now, you could probably live off the interest alone and provide enough for the baby's college fund." Hartford agent stated

"Thank you so much for taking an interest in my case. I would not have known what to do with handling such an amount." Chris was grateful.

"We are done with the transaction. You should be receiving a statement within the next ten business days, summarizing the entire transactions between my company and Fidelity. I wish you and your baby the very best in life. Here is my card, if you have any questions. Have a good day." Hartford agent did the handshake

"You too, have a good day. Thank you again." Chris and the baby walked the Hartford agent to the door.

It has been an exciting day. She would trade her wealth in a heartbeat to have Mark by her side. The baby was due for his feeding. Chris took the baby in the living room to sit by the fireplace while she breastfed him. She was telling the baby stories of how she met his daddy, how they fell in love and described his daddy's best qualities. When the baby finally fell asleep, Chris started crying and said, "Oh, Mark, I miss you so much. You promised me that you would be back for us. You did not keep your promise. I do not know how to go on without you. Our son keeps me going. We will be moving soon to our blue house. It is there that I feel you most." Chris was in tears as she slowly rocked her baby.

CHAPTER 13

COMING HOME TO CRYSTAL COVE ISLAND

The move to Crystal Cove went as planned. Tom and Marie accompanied Chris and the baby to the island. When Tom and Marie stepped off the ferry, they felt the peace and tranquility immediately. They both loved the house, even though the house was somewhat cluttered with boxes and some of the furniture were not in their places yet. Despite the "overcrowding," Tom and Marie felt very much at home. It was cozy and homey, which is how Mark would have liked it. Having Tom and Marie there to help Chris, the house became more and more heart-warming.

"Do you guys have any plans for Thanksgiving this year? If not, would you like to spend it with us, here in Crystal Cove Island?" Chris asked.

"You do not have to ask us twice. Marie, what do you think?" Tom turned to Marie to ask.

"I would love it. You might not be able to get rid of us. From what I have seen in the travel brochures, the island is a place to see the most spectacular holiday decorations from Thanksgiving until a week after the New Year. I have seen some postcards from this place. They are simply beautiful and lovely surroundings. Hey, Tom, what do you think about moving here?" Marie was excited about Chris' invitation.

"That would be a dream and a lovely thought. I do not think we could afford such a place, with my retirement, but at least we know someone that lives here to visit." Tom seemed disappointed.

"That is what Mark and I said until we looked at this house. Some properties are still affordable. That would be neat, if we became neighbors, again." Chris could only wish they would move to the island.

"That would be a dream. Oh, well, we could only imagine, but eventually, reality would hit us like a ton of bricks. Now, that we know you live here, this can be our "getaway" location." Marie said

Tom and Marie stayed for a couple of days to help Chris with unpacking and helped with arranging her furniture. They returned home; the house was quiet. The next morning was sunny but a little chilly. Chris bundled the baby and decided to go for a stroll down the neighborhood, hoping to meet some of her neighbors. As they walked out the gate, she saw her next-door neighbor having tea or coffee on the porch. They waved at her, and she waved back. Both women walked over to the gate seemingly wanting to invite Chris to meet her.

"Hello, there. Welcome to the neighborhood. My name is Betty, and this is my sister, Carla. Who is this in the carriage?" Betty was cheerful when she greeted Chris and the baby. Carla was a bit shyer she just waved.

"My name is Christina Jensen, but you can call me Chris. My son, Benjamin-Mark is in the carriage. We just moved in last week, just the two of us living next door. The baby must like the fresh air; he is asleep again." Chris introduced herself and her son.

"How old is he?" Betty asked.

"He will be three months old in a week, born a day after Labor Day," Chris answered. She went on to say, "We are from Seattle area, Everett to be exact.

"My sister and I have lived here for 45 years. We were both schoolteachers until ten years ago when we retired. We are just about to have some tea and crumpets, would you like to join us?" Betty asked

"That sounds lovely, yes. Wow, I can see why you have been here for a while. I love it here too. I detect a slight accent. Where are you two from?" Chris asked

"My sister and I came to this island from England as a tourist. We loved it so much due to the simplicity and unhurried lifestyle we decided to stay. How do you take your tea?" Betty asked

"Just plain tea would be great, thank you. I noticed that there are not too many people out and about, do they keep to themselves?" Chris was curious

"It is different on weekends. Most people work and live in Seattle area during the week, and they come home to Crystal Cove to have peace and quiet. The rest are either retired or work for the state, school or the tourist industry." Carla spoke so gently.

After they finished their tea and crumpets, Chris wanted to complete the block or save the other side of the block for another day. "Thank you so much for the tea and crumpets. I enjoyed the visit and meeting you two. See you soon." Chris waved back at Betty and Carla.

Chris and the baby continued their walk to the end of the block before crossing the other side of the street, to see who else might be outside. When they got to the middle of the block, a man happened to be chopping wood. Chris just waved at the man, with no intention to interrupt his work. However, he ran over to Chris to stop them and meet the new neighbor. He got closer to where Chris was standing.

"Hello, you must be the new neighbor across the street. My name is Adam Harrison." Adam greeted them,

"Hello…" Chris returned the greetings.

As he got closer, Chris noticed his piercing blue eyes, which reminded her of another first meeting she encountered. A flash down memory lane of her initial meeting with Mark came to mind suddenly. She could not help but stare at him until she noticed Adam was waiting for a response from her.

"I am sorry for staring. I did not mean to interrupt your work. We were just out for a stroll enjoying the beautiful day, hoping to meet some of the neighbors. My name is Christina Jensen, but you can call me Chris. We just moved in last week. My house is that blue one just across the street." Chris pointed out her home.

"Welcome to the neighborhood. Hope, you will like it here. Who is in the buggy?" Adam asked.

"My son, Benjamin-Mark is in the buggy. He happens to be asleep at the moment. He seems to like the fresh, clean air. He has been asleep

since we started our stroll. Maybe, you can meet him when he is awake."
Chris said

"What a nice name, Benjamin-Mark. How did he inherit the
name?" Adam asked

"I have always liked the name Benjamin or Ben, so it stuck with
me. His full name is Benjamin Mark. I think it is a beautiful name for
a boy." Chris was so proud to say his full name.

"How old is your boy?" Adam was curious

"He was born the day after Labor Day, so that makes him almost
three months old." She said

"Oh, my, he is just a young man. I bet his dad cannot wait until he
is old enough to play ball." Adam commented

"We better let you go on with your work. It looks like you have a
lot to do." Chris quickly responded.

"Do you need some firewood? I would be more than happy to
share some of these. I have much more wood to chop in the backyard. I
usually give them away to my neighbors. Now, that you live across the
street, you qualify for free wood. "Adam was being neighborly.

"I will take you up on that offer, thank you. I think I have enough
for this week, so there is no rush in my case. I can wait," Chris was
grateful.

"Okay, I will add you to my list. If I may be bold for a second, but
if you cook me a meal, I will double your wood delivery." Adam boldly
stated

"Well, thank you, I will keep that in mind. Enjoy the rest of your
day. See you around." Chris continued the walk home. The short time
she spent with Adam, she felt a connection that only happened once.
Chris and the baby walked the entire block, waving at other neighbors.
She was able to meet another retired couple, the Miller's, who happened
to be just leaving for doctor's appointment. So far, the people on the
block have been accommodating. She hopes to meet the others soon.
Baby Ben was still sleeping when they got in the house. Chris put him
down in his crib. There was a slight chill in the house, so she threw in
a couple of logs in the fireplace. She made a cup of tea and brought it
out on the porch. From a distance, Adam was still chopping wood. He

waved at her, and she waved back. Adam started to walk towards her house, with a cart full of wood.

"Hello, again, you could never have too much firewood. I have to stack them somewhere. I might as well stack it here. Where would you like me to stack the wood?" Adam asked

"Right in that corner would be just fine. Thank you so much. Can I offer you some tea or water to drink? I also have fresh lemonade, if you like." Chris made the offer

"Lemonade sounds good if it is not too much trouble." He said

"Let me get the lemonade. Here you go." She said

"Thank you. This lemonade is refreshing, and it hit the spot." Adam said

"How long have you lived here on this island?" Chris asked

"I have been here less than a year. As the saying goes, they made me a lucrative offer to take early "retirement" from a very boring job, so I took the offer. I wanted to work outdoors, doing mindless jobs. Here I am, chopping wood that pays virtually nil, but at least, I can breathe the fresh air, not feel suffocated in the corporate office setting. What about you, what brought you here?" he asked

"It is a long story. Let us save it for another day. My son will be waking up soon. I will need to feed him and bathe him. Thank you again for the wood." She said

"You are welcome. Thank you for the drink. See you around." Adam said

Adam continued to supply Chris with firewood. He had been stacking the wood on Chris' porch very neatly; often Chris would come out to thank him with either a cup of coffee or something to drink. From time to time, they would exchange waves when they see each other from a distance.

CHAPTER 14

THE HOLIDAYS

The month of November has been a busy one for Chris. She accomplished her mission to meeting most of her neighbors on the block. Everyone welcomed her and the baby. Often, she would fine homemade cookies, cakes, flowers, jams-jellies, etc. delivered at the front door. Others would leave notes, offering their services to watch the baby if she needs to run errands. Surrounded by such good neighbors, she feels very safe in her home.

Thanksgiving happens to be only a week away. It is a painful reminder that she will be celebrating a major holiday without Mark. Thank goodness, Tom and Marie from the "apartment days" in Everett will be coming soon to Crystal Cove to spend their first Thanksgiving with her and the baby. Excited to host a Thanksgiving dinner at her home, Chris decorated the house in fall colors. In between the baby's nap time, she would be baking cookies or pies. To avoid the last-minute rush, Chris ordered the turkey and dressing ahead of time at a local grocery store. All she had to do on Thursday was to pick up the turkey in the morning and put it in the oven for about four hours. The morning of Thanksgiving Day, Chris woke up early to do last minute preparation. The baby was still asleep when she checked in on him. When the baby woke up, Chris bundled him up so that they can pick up the turkey and dressing. As they walked into the grocery store, Adam was just coming in. He helped her with the door, and they exchanged greetings. Adam came in to pick up just a few items and pick up one turkey dinner. The butcher told him he would have to come back later because they have not prepared the individual dinners. He ran into Chris as he was leaving and asked her if she needed some assistance with carrying out her groceries. She thanked him for his offer, but it was not necessary. One of the workers at the store would help her with putting the groceries in her golf cart. While waiting for the butcher, Mr. Allison, to wrap up her order, he started a conversation with her. Mr. Allison, well liked and well known by just about everyone in town provided the latest gossip. Not only does he know the "special meat of the day" and how to cook any cut of meat, he knows the latest town gossip. He mentioned to Chris that Adam ordered only one turkey dinner for Thanksgiving as he placed the big turkey and dressing in her cart. When she got back from the store, Adam happened to be stacking the firewood on the porch. By the front door was a beautiful floral arrangement of wildflowers in a very lovely homemade vase.

"Hey, there, thank you for the firewood. Did you bring the flowers? They are beautiful. Thank you. It will be a perfect centerpiece for the dinner table." Chris admired the flowers and very appreciative of Adam's thoughtfulness and kindness.

"You are welcome. It looks like you need some help with your groceries. Let me get them." Adam saw that Chris was holding the baby and she needed a hand with her bags.

"By the way, do you have any plans for dinner tonight? A couple of my closest friends from Seattle will be arriving soon to spend Thanksgiving with us. We have plenty of food for about a dozen people. Would you like to join us?" Chris was hoping he would accept the invitation.

"Thank you for the invitation, but you are not obligated to invite me because I brought you wood and flowers. Besides, what will your friends think when they see a strange man in your home so soon?" Adam did not want to sound too ungrateful for the invitation, but he was more concern about her friends seeing him at the dinner table.

"I appreciate your concern for my reputation, but my friends have known me a long time to think differently of me because I have a male friend. How is that different from having a female friend for dinner? Feel free to bring a date or anyone you would like to bring with you.

Please, come and join us." Chris explained and hoped he accepts the invitation to dinner so that he can meet her friends.

"It would only be me. I am a bit of a loner, so I do not have a date to bring. Are you sure about having a complete stranger at your dinner table with your friends?" Adam wanted to give her another chance to reconsider.

"No more excuses. Be here around five o'clock pm for cocktails. I will be disappointed if you are a no-show. "Chris was not going to accept no for an answer.

"I will be there. Can I bring anything else?" Adam asked

"Nope, you already brought me firewood and gorgeous flowers. See you later." Chris said.

Chris occasionally looked out the front door for Tom and Marie. She saw a golf cart approaching her house with more than just two people. As they got closer, she was pleasantly surprised and happy to see Sandy, Lorraine, and Pete with them. It is like old times in the apartment complex when they would celebrate holidays together. She forgot that she only has enough chairs for six people. After they greeted each other and let them in the house, she quickly walked over to Adam's house to ask if he would bring a couple of extra chairs. Her friends from the apartment complex simply could not say enough good things about her adorable home. From the street to the house, the lantern of real pumpkins lined the pathway to the door, a pile of cornhusks in the garden area, and a cornucopia of fall harvest adorned the porch to the entrance of the house, extending to the living room/kitchen area. The dinner table, complete with elegant China dishes, crystal glasses, and fine silverware, looked festive and perfect for the Thanksgiving occasion. The bouquet of wildflowers that Adam brought completed a very elegant table setting with country flair. Tom brought a couple of bottles of wine made and bottled from Bellingham Washington. He opened up the bottles of wine for quick sampling. Before Adam was due to arrive, Chris gave them a heads up information on Adam. Not that she needed to explain, but she stated Adam was originally from back East and did not have any family members nearby, so she invited him to dinner to meet her dear friends. Adam knocked at the door, carrying a couple of chairs. Chris introduced him to everyone. They welcomed him and made him feel like he is one of them. Sandy immediately took a liking to Adam, so she switched the name tag next to Adam. Everyone was having a good time, catching up with one another, asking Adam lots of questions. With all the laughter and conversations going on in the dining room, the baby woke up and started crying. Chris brought him out and introduced him as the 'man of the house.' The little guy dressed in a pilgrim outfit looked so cute, they all wanted to hold him including Adam. All the times he has been over to deliver wood, the baby was always asleep. That was the first time he has seen the baby awake. He could not wait to hold him.

"Let us all take a seat at the table and hold hands as we say a short prayer. Marie, would you like to lead us in a prayer. Tom, since you brought the wine would you be our bartender and Pete would you help Tom with the drinks for everybody. Lorraine and Sandy, would you please help me put the rest of the food on the table." Chris requested.

Marie said the prayer then, Chris added how grateful to be with her dearest friends at the table, while she silently thought of Mark. After the prayer, everyone did their assigned task and took their seat around the table. Sandy started to dish out the mashed potatoes, gravy, while Lorraine handled the yams, bean casserole, corn and brussel sprouts. Adam carved the turkey as each requested dark or white meat. They continued eating, laughing, talking, just having a good time with friends including Adam. It was time for dessert. The choices were pumpkin pie, apple, pecan, and of course vanilla ice cream.

"Lorraine, would you help me with the dessert request. Your choices are pumpkin, apple, or pecan pies. There is vanilla ice cream or whip cream, coffee, tea or other drinks are also in the offering. Pete, would you serve the drinks, please." Chris asked for assistance as she was holding the baby.

"Of course, I will get it started." Pete complied

"I am not much for dessert. Chris, may I hold the baby so that you can enjoy your dessert? I will just sit in the rocking chair." Adam asked

"Are you sure, you do not want any dessert? We have ice cream." Chris suggested

"I am sure. I may have ice cream later. Would you trust me with your son?" Adam asked to hold the baby.

"Of course, he is going to need a bottle shortly, so go ahead and take a seat in the rocking chair. Here he is, and I will get the bottle." Chris was surprised Adam wanted to hold the baby.

Adam was careful holding baby Ben. Chris brought the bottle that she had warmed up. He looked very natural holding and feeding the baby while everyone had their dessert. Chris could not help but notice how comfortable he was holding the baby. He even knew how to burp him after he finished the bottle. Adam was enjoying his time in the rocking chair to everyone's surprise.

"Adam, you looked like a pro at handling the baby. Have you done this before? It looks like he is asleep. I will take him so that I can put him down on his bed." Chris commented as she saw how tenderly he handled baby Ben.

"You can show me his room, and I will put him down. I have younger siblings that I took care of when they were younger. I was an excellent sitter." Adam commented

"Okay, let me show you his room." Chris agreed

"Not to change the subject, but I have a couple of spare bedrooms available for your guests if you need them," Adam suggested

"Adam, I like that idea. Are you sure about that? I was only expecting Tom and Marie, but I am glad to see the others. Okay, I will make that suggestion. Thank you for offering your home to my friends you just met a few hours ago. It will probably be more comfortable than the couch or the floor. Tom and Marie can stay with me. Let us get back to my guest." Relieved that Adam offered his home, she accepted his offering.

"Hey, everyone, Adam offered his house for better accommodations than my couch or the floor. I only have one spare bedroom, sorry." Chris announced

"Since our luggage is in your guest room, Marie and I will take that room, if that is okay with everyone," Tom claimed the room immediately.

"My offering includes breakfast. I can make decent breakfast, so breakfast is on me. I am also volunteering to be your tour guide if you all want to see the island. What do you say? Adam suggested. He added, "The downtown area will be in full holiday decor, and the stores will be open until midnight." Adam said

"Gosh, Adam, I did not expect this. Thank you for volunteering.

Yes, we will take you up on your offer. The tour downtown should get you in the holiday spirit. It will be a lot of fun. Take lots of pictures." Chris was delighted with Adam's suggestions. She kept thinking Mark would be handling all that if he were alive.

Due to safety policy, babies in car seats cannot ride on golf carts for long distance trips. Chris and the baby will not be able to go on the island tour with the rest of them, which was fine with Chris. She needed to do some cleaning up and put away the food, dishes, etc. Fortunately, Adam was available to give them the tour of the island. Chris and Sandy were in the kitchen cleaning the table.

"What a nice man, Adam. Is he single?" Sandy asked

"Just before I asked him to join us for Thanksgiving dinner, I told him he could bring a date. He said he did not have a significant other to bring and that he is a bit of a loner, whatever that means. He is very nice, kind, thoughtful and has a charming personality. Are you interested?" Chris asked

"Yeah, you know me so well, always looking. He has that gentleness about him that is very attractive." Sandy said with great interest. Chris could not agree more.

"Well, Sandy here is your chance to make the connection. He is one of a kind that you don't meet very often." Chris added.

The following morning they gathered at Adam's house for breakfast. He made old-fashioned pancakes, bacon, eggs, hash-browns and cut-up fresh fruits. Everyone complimented Adam with how great of a host he was and also a good cook. He blushed when he heard the compliments from Chris' friends. Adam picked up a golf cart big enough to seat all of them. They all fit comfortably in one golf cart. Adam did not want to leave Chris and the baby behind, but he knew the high risk of tipping over on golf carts. Chris and baby watched as they embarked on their tour. They probably will not be back until dinnertime. In between baby naps, Chris was able to prepare new food using the leftovers. She made a couple of casserole dishes, simple enough to bake in the oven when they arrive.

The "tour group" began their journey by admiring the nearby houses decorated beautifully; no ornaments or lights left unused from any of the homes. Every home had at least one decorated Christmas tree in front of the house. It is a picture perfect site to get anyone into a holiday mood. When they reached the downtown area, they saw the sidewalks lined with entertainers and carolers that make anyone want to join in singing a chorus or two of Christmas songs. Adam attempted to take them to the Crystal Cove Vineyard, but the streets were closed for golf carts, open only for foot traffic. They opted to save the tour to the vineyard for next time. The tour group got back to Chris' house just before it got dark. They can smell the aroma of home cooking coming from the kitchen. Chris and the baby were sitting in the rocking chair in front of the fireplace when they all arrived. Everyone took turns telling Chris how much fun they had touring the island, each one sharing their favorite sights, store, street scene, or the overall experience on the island. Shopping bags, artifacts, souvenirs filled almost the entire living room, making it look like a department store.

When the buzzer from the oven began to go off, they started towards the dinner table, where Chris had already set up the place settings for everyone. Adam went to get more firewood to keep the cozy warm fire going. When he got back, he asked Chris if he could hold the baby to give her a break and mingle with her friends as she prepared dinner. She handed her bundle of joy to Adam, knowing that he is capable of handling babies. Still, she was pleasantly surprised that he takes an interest in handling the baby instead of mingling with others. Chris welcomed the break.

"It has been one of the most wonderful Thanksgiving weekends we have been. Pete and I would like to come back on Christmas and stay at one of that Bed and Breakfast in town. Do you have any recommendations on which Bed and Breakfast would be best?" Lorraine asked

"I have only stayed at Crystal Cove Inn. I recommend that place very highly. Adam, you have lived here longer than I have, which one would you recommend?" Chris turned to Adam to ask

"I would have to agree with you on the Crystal Cove Inn. The rooms are very well color coordinated. It is like having Martha Stuart personally add her touch on every item in the rooms. All the rooms have a huge fireplace, which you will enjoy as you watch the fresh snow falling outside. Each unit has a spectacular view of the water, sunrise/

sunset, and part of the downtown area. They serve free breakfast, with the homemade menu. They also have their own restaurant, where they have just about anything fresh and homemade. You cannot go wrong with your choice." Adam was describing the Inn in details.

"You sound like you have stayed there before. From the way you describe it, you have fond memories of the place." Pete teased Adam to get a reaction from him.

"Yes, I have stayed at the Inn before, but you cannot get me to "kiss and tell." Adam teased them back.

Everyone was chuckling, hoping to get Adam out of his shell. He fits right in and enjoying the friendly bantering from the people he just met twenty-four hours ago. Chris paused for a moment, thinking about Adam's comments on the rooms at the Inn. The words he used were so similar to her own words she used when she and Mark stayed at the Inn. It brought back some memories she shared with the man she loved.

"Are you all hungry? Dinner is almost ready. Tom, will be our bartender, again, please. In addition to wine, we have ice tea, soda, lemonade, sparkling water. Marie, you can be Tom's assistant. The cups and glasses are up in the cupboards. Sandy, if you would help me with getting out the casseroles from the oven that would be great. Let us gather around the table. I would like to start out with a small blessing, thanking the Almighty Father for the bountiful food and having great friends at the table, Amen." Chris said. She saw how well they all worked together.

After dinner, they relaxed around the living room with some music. Tom started the trend of slow dancing with Marie. The rest followed suit. Sandy asked Adam to dance. Chris has the baby as her partner. They traded partners when the music changed. Marie offered to hold the baby, so Chris was free to dance. She danced with Tom, Pete, and finally with Adam. Adam was pleased to dance with Chris finally. He traditionally held her, making sure he was proper even though he wanted to hold her closer. They locked eyes for a moment but quickly turned away. She let go of Adam before the music ended. She walked over to Marie to get her little man back. It had been a long day, so they started to wind down and went to their designated room. The following morning, Adam fixed everyone breakfast before heading back to the ferry landing. They said their goodbyes to Chris and the baby. Adam took them to the ferry landing.

After Adam dropped Chris' friends to the ferry terminal, he returned to Chris' house to check on her and ask if she needed any assistance with cleaning up. Chris just put the baby down for a nap when he came knocking.

"Hi Adam, come in. I just put the baby down for a nap. Would you like something to drink? It is almost lunchtime. How would you like a sandwich? The choices are ham, turkey or a combination." Chris asked as they walked towards the kitchen.

"I will have a ham sandwich, please," Adam said

"By the way, my friends wanted me to thank you for your hospitality and making them feel welcomed. You were a hit! They are looking forward to a return visit to Crystal Cove, especially Sandy. Don't be surprised if she calls you." Chris mentioned Sandy to get his reaction.

"You have such wonderful friends. I am glad to have met them. This, Thanksgiving, tops any other holidays I have had in a long time. Thank you, for including me amongst your closest circle of friends." Adam thoroughly enjoyed the time with Chris' friends.

"You were a life-saver. I should be thanking you for coming to my rescue. You provided lodging, meals and took them on tour of the island. Thank you, for your kind hospitality and friendship. All my friends just love you." Chris sincerely thanked Adam for being such a good neighbor.

"Would you like to eat at the dining table or out on the porch?" Chris asked

"It might be a little chilly for you out on the porch. I think right here would be fine. Would you like me to help you fix the sandwiches or bring out the drinks?" Adam asked

Chris made several sandwiches while Adam took out and served the freshly made lemonade that has become his favorite drink. He took a couple of steps away from the fridge when he lightly collided with Chris carrying a tray of sandwiches. To prevent her from falling, he grabbed her by the waist with his free hand. He pulled her close to him to hold her steady until she gets her footing. They both stared at each other for a couple of seconds before he let her go.

"I am sorry Chris for not looking where I was going. Are you okay?" he asked

"It was my fault. I turned too quickly. I am fine now." Chris said

Adam let her go. They both let out a chuckle before they took their seat on the table. They proceeded to eat their lunch. In the meantime, Adam thought about how close he held Chris, and the subtle fragrance of her perfume lingered in his mind.

"Did you have a nice visit with your friends?" Adam started the conversation.

"They surprised me when they all came to visit. It was like old times at the apartment complex. I miss them already." Chris thought about Mark at that moment saddened her

"Say, Christmas and New Years are coming up. It is the most spectacular and festive time of the year here on the island; not a single Christmas light left unused." He said, hoping that would cheer her up.

"My sister who lives in San Diego asked if we would come down for Christmas. We have some families there that would like to see the baby. It sounded like a good idea." Chris responded

"Oh, you are going away for Christmas? For sure, it would be warmer in San Diego than here," he said

"Would you like some tea?" Chris asked

"Yes, I would love some tea with just honey, please," he said

Chris remembered that Mark takes his tea with only honey, but a million others also take their tea with honey, no big deal. She asked, "What are your plans for Christmas?"

"Most of my families are back east. I will likely have dinner with Betty and Carla on Christmas day. They usually invite several neighbors to have Christmas dinner with them." Adam replied

Chris started to get the tea kettle ready when baby Ben started to wake up. It is almost time for his feeding. Adam got up right away.

"Would you like me to pick him up?" Adam anxiously asked

Adam went into the baby's room to get him. He said, "Hey, little guy. Are you hungry? You sure are a handsome boy. Mommy just made sandwiches. Would you like a sandwich?" he kiddingly asked

"He is probably hungry. Let me take him so that I can feed my little guy.

Chris and the baby sat on the rocking chair in the living room while she breastfeeds the baby. Adam stayed in the kitchen to keep an eye on the hot water boiling on the stove. He also wanted to give Chris the privacy while she breastfed the baby. After the baby was fed and burped, he went back to sleep.

CHAPTER 15

CHRISTINA'S STORY

Chris and Adam brought their drinks on the porch. The sun was still shining so brightly, but a little chilly. Ben brought out a small lap blanket for Chis to put around her shoulders.

"It is nice out here. The sandwich sure hit the spot." Mark said

"Let me just check on the baby and bring the monitor out here," Chris said. She came back out and sat the monitor down next to her.

"Is everything all right?" Adam asked. Chris just nodded her head. He went on to ask, "May I ask what made you move here to Crystal Cove?"

"It is a long story," Chris said

"I have the time, if you are willing to tell the story, I would like to hear it." Adam quickly responded.

"Believe it or not, I came to Crystal Cove Island after reading about a small vineyard on the back of a wine bottle. You know the vineyard." Chris said

"Yes, it is quite a legend that most people who have lived here on the island talk about it to this day. It is a must- see the site here on the island. I attempted to take your friends there, but due to the enormous crowd around the lookout during Thanksgiving weekend we were unable to get to it. They said it would be a reason to come back to the island to see the vineyard. Let me know when you want to go there, and I will take you." Adam answered

"I will take you up on that offer after the holiday rush." she said

"I didn't mean to interrupt your story, please, go on," he said

"As I was saying, I came to Crystal Cove Island after a major breakup that nearly destroyed my confidence as a woman. At the same time, my boss highly recommended me for job change that would require strong leadership and extensive work experience to become a Director in the Human Resources Department. Drowning in self-doubt, lacking a sense of direction and not having the confidence of functioning as a leader, I could not consider accepting the job offer. Then, a perfect stranger came into my life, saving me from self-destruction and changing my life forever." Chris stopped for a moment to look at Adam and see how intrigued he seemed to be while listening to her story. He encouraged her to go on.

"Please, go on, unless you want to keep the rest of your story private. I can accept that." Adam explained

"He came into my life just in the nick of time. He moved to Everett, Washington after being in Europe for five years, and worked as an independent contractor working for the U.S. Government. I invited him to Crystal Cove, not for any romantic interlude, but because he made me feel safe and respected. I did not see it at the time the genuine love he felt for me because my head was full of self-doubt and my heart left broken. I did not want to admit my feelings thinking that I do not deserve such a good man whose only fault was being in love with me. Adam, do you believe in destiny?" Chris asked Adam.

"Yes, I do believe in destiny. So, what happened to the man that came into your life? What made you come back to Crystal Cove Island to live here? " Adam asked with such curiosity.

"His line of work required a lot of traveling. Later on in our relationship, the travels became more frequent, and the duration seemed longer. He soon realized that he wanted a more traditional life for us, so he decided to leave his job and settle down. The U.S. Government requested one last assignment that will take only one year to complete. He asked me to give him one year, with a promise to come back to me and live happily ever after. He broke his promise." Tears started streaming down her face before Chris can finish her sentence.

"Chris, I am sorry this is upsetting to you. You do not need to say anymore. Let us change the subject, what do you say?" Adam suggested. He wanted to hold her and comfort her, but it would not be appropriate at this time.

"No, I need to tell the story because it gives me great comfort knowing that his spirit is all around my baby and me. Just being in our home, which he bought for us during our visit on the island, is where I feel him the most, and he is watching over us. Give me a few minutes to compose my thoughts." Chris asked

"Okay, as long as you want to continue, I am here to listen," Adam said

"Mark will always be the love of my life even though he was not able to keep his promise to come back to me after his one-year tour. He was a casualty of war in the Middle East just before his son was born. The U.S. Government did not officially notify me of his death because we were not legally married except for the simple ceremony we had at Crystal Cove Island, the small chapel near the lighthouse. He paid a heavy price for me to own this house that he promised we would raise our family together and grow old forever." Chris started crying uncontrollably as she talked about Mark lovingly.

"Oh, Chris, I am so sorry." Adam held her close to console her. He stroked her head and kissed her forehead. He tried to wipe the tears from her face. This time, he kissed her on the lips. She kissed him back. He pulled away quickly when he realized what was happening. He stood up and looked away from her. He turned around to face her.

"Chris, I should not have done that, kiss you." Adam felt embarrassed

"No, it's okay. It is okay." Chris tried to convince Adam in a soft voice. This was the first time she felt Mark was kissing her. She can smell his scent and feel his touches, which she has not felt since their last time together. She did not want him to stop.

"Chris, your love story is so beautiful and fascinating." Adam could only think how he can relate to her story. He went on to say, "I am sure he did everything within his power to keep his promise to you. It sounds like part of you died with him. You are a beautiful, young woman, who will make another man very happy to have you. Why do you give up so easily? You have his son; he would want you to go on. I am certain of that." Adam hoped to convince Chris.

"That is weird. I have heard those similar words from Mark in one of our serious conversations. Now, I hear it from you. I know I do not want to love another man that way again. I would be forsaking his love and dishonoring his memory. Right now, I only have one man to love, and that is my son. I hope and pray that I could be a good parent to him. I am looking forward to raising my son the best way I know how; spare him from disappointments and heartaches, if I can help it." Chris felt passionate about her statement,

"This man of yours, who was not able to keep his promise to you, must have a darn good reason why he was not able to deliver the goods. He was lucky to have found a woman who continues to love him as you do. I cannot see him wanting you to be alone just because he is not around. Do you want more kids?" Adam implored.

"I am not alone. I have my son. Yes, I would like to have more children, but now we cannot." She said it convincingly.

"He sounds like an honorable and unselfish being. I am certain he would want you to go on with your life and be happy." Adam persisted, but he sensed he could not convince Chris. She was staring at the horizon, seemingly a million miles away. He excused himself and said, "On that note, I should go. You do not need any more unsolicited advice from me. Thank you again for the most enjoyable Thanksgiving weekend in a long time. See you around."

The following weeks after Thanksgiving, she saw Adam from a distance. They would wave at each other and go about their business. It seems unusual that Adam had not come over for a visit as if he was avoiding seeing Chris. The wood supply seems bottomless, always full. He has been delivering the wood very early in the morning. Previously, Adam would deliver the wood when he sees her up and around, his excuse to come over. She misses the interaction she had with Adam. What is it about Adam's presence that makes Mark's memories nearer? A week before Chris and the baby were set to fly down to San Diego; Adam came over to offer his service to take them to the airport. He knocked at the door, but no answer.

"Knock, knock. Chris, are you home?" Adam said aloud.

"Yeah, Adam, just wait a second." She hollered from the baby's room.

"Hey, stranger, I just put the baby down for his nap. What brings you here?" she asked. Adam was standing just on the other side of the screen door.

"I know you are leaving for San Diego for the holidays. I was just wondering if you needed a ride to the airport." Adam asked.

"You must be psychic. I was thinking about the same thing. It is a little difficult to travel with the baby. Come on in. Would you like something to drink or eat? Chris asked

"No, thank you. I am okay right now. I just stopped in to offer assistance on your trip down to San Diego." Adam replied as he was coming in the door.

"I was just about to look into the different transportations available to get to the airport. It is not so easy to travel with the baby by myself, so many things to pack for such a little person. I think your offer is the best by far, that is if the offer is still good." Chris asked

"I could bring you both to the airport so that it would be easier for you and the baby. The weather has been unpredictable lately. I would like to take you both to the airport and pick you both up when you return." Adam simply stated.

"I accept your offer, thank you. Are you sure?" She asked again

"Yes, I would like to," Adam assured her.

"There is a slight change in the trip to San Diego. My sister met someone she really likes. He invited her to go on a New Year's Eve cruise to the Bahamas. She sounds so excited about this man. Since she is going to be gone starting New Year's Eve, the baby and I are coming home early and be home for New Year's." Chris explained the change

For a moment there, Adam was not sure if he heard it right, that Chris and the baby were going to be home before New Year's Eve. He was excited at the possibility of spending New Years with the two of them.

"Would you leave me a copy of your itinerary to be sure I have the times and flights correct?" Adam requested

"I happen to have a copy here, and I wrote down my sister's phone number. I am also leaving you a spare key to my house, "she noted

When Adam came to the door to take Chris and the baby to the airport, he saw what a struggle she would have to go through traveling by herself with the baby. He took them all the way to the ticket counter so that she can check in the luggage and the stroller. Chris had a front pack to carry baby in front, her purse on one arm and a diaper bag on the other arm. They were getting ready to board the plane.

"Oh, my, will you be able to handle all of that? Have a great Christmas with your family, and I will see you two when you get back. Call me when you get in San Diego." Adam wished he was going too. He hugged her and kissed her on the cheek. He also kissed the baby on the forehead before saying goodbye. One of the flight attendants helped her with her bags. Adam watched as they turned the corner to get on the plane and waved.

After Adam dropped Chris and the baby at the Seattle airport, the drive back to Crystal Cove seemed wearisome and endless. He missed them already. Adam spent Christmas day with Betty and Carla. They had dinner together, exchanged gifts, and visited for a while. Adam's thoughts were on Chris and the baby, imagining them sitting around the Christmas tree, opening their presents.

"Where are Chris and the baby spending their Christmas?" Betty asked

"They went down to San Diego to visit her sister. They have not seen the baby, so she decided to go down there. They will be back before New Year's." Adam answered

"She seems like a very nice young woman, someone that should be with a man like you. You two make a very nice couple. We see how you two interact with one another. I think you two like each other but do not know it. Am I right?" Carla was making an observation comment.

"Oh, Carla, you are a hopeless romantic. We are just good friends. Although I like the idea, she is not ready for any romantic relationship. She is still in love with a man, who is also the father of her baby. From what I can gather, he was killed in the Middle East, working for the U.S. Government at the time. It is a fascinating love story that she would not mind sharing with you if you ask. One thing I am certain of, she has come to love Crystal Cove and people like you that she will stay for a long time, at least I hope so." Adam commented

"Do not give up on her. She will come around when her heart is ready. "Betty added

"Just between the three of us, I intend to do just that. I have never felt this way about someone so quickly. I want her to want me as much as I want to be with her." he said

"It sounds like you are speaking from the heart. You must love her very much that you are willing to give her the time and space until she realizes how she feels." Betty commented.

Betty could not have been more forthright about her comment. Adam could only return a smile, knowing he knew the truth. Carla nodded her head in agreement with Betty's statement.

Just a couple of more days before Chris and the baby were scheduled to come home. Adam has been looking forward to this day. While they were gone, he made a dressing table for the baby, made out of oak wood from his trees in the backyard. The dressing table will come in handy for Chris to dress and change the baby in a more comfortable level than having to bend down on the floor. He added drawers within easy reach for diapers, clothes and miscellaneous items for the baby. He personalized the dressing table by carving *Benjamin-Mark* on the front side. It would be an heirloom that baby Ben could pass on to his children. He brought it in the house and placed it next to the crib. The two pieces looked like a set of "country oak" baby furniture. To welcome them back, he prepped the house with some pine wreaths and cedar cones in the fireplace. The fragrance of fresh pines made the house smelling like the fresh outdoors. He even made a shepherd's pie for dinner, with homemade gravy and green beans ready to be placed in the oven. In his excitement to see Chris and the baby, he left early for the airport to pick them up. He spotted them right away as the last passengers off the plane. Chris waved and smiled at Adam the moment she saw him. The flight attendant helped her with the baby and her belongings. Adam walked up to Chris as she handed the baby to him so that she can take her purse and bag from the flight attendant. He was more than happy to hold the baby. He missed this little guy. Chris, glad to see Adam, gave him a hug and a kiss on the cheeks. She almost kissed him on the lips, but caught herself and just looked away. When they got to Chris' house, the fragrance of fresh pine in the house was an indication that they were home. Adam put on a couple of logs in the fireplace to warm up the house. The baby fell asleep, so Chris put him down in his crib. She noticed right away the beautiful, new dressing table next to the crib. She went over to where Adam was at, who was in the kitchen getting ready to put the shepherd's pie in the oven. She hugged him from behind. She caught him by surprise that he almost dropped the dish. He turned around to return the hug, and she immediately buried her face in his chest as tears streamed down her face.

"What is this about? Why are you crying?" Adam was curious at her actions.

Chris could not say how she felt. He just held her in his arms. She finally lifted her head from his chest to graciously acknowledge the thoughtfulness by making an heirloom dressing table for her son.

"The dressing table is beautiful. What a gift to give to my son. You honored his life by making a beautiful piece of furniture with his name engraved on it. It will be a keepsake for him to pass on to his son. You touched my heart by the thoughtfulness you put into making the table. Thank you..." Chris was sincerely emotional by what he did.

"I am glad you like it. It helped me pass the time away. Are you hungry? I was just about to put dinner in the oven." Adam asked

"Yes, I am hungry. You have thought of everything. Tell me, did you bake an apple pie for dessert?" Chris was just kidding, trying to get a reaction from him.

"I am sorry; I did not make any dessert. If you like, I can quickly go to the grocery store and pick one up." Adam replied

"Gosh, no desserts, what kind of restaurant are you running here? Just kidding...," she was just teasing Adam knowing he does not like dessert. Adam took out the shepherd's pie. She commented, "Wow! This shepherd's pie looks homemade. Did you make it? How long should I put it in the oven? It looks like you have some fresh vegetables. Do you just want me to steam them with some butter?" she asked

"That sounds good. By the way, your boy seems to have grown a lot in just a couple of weeks." Adam commented

"Let me just check on the baby. It is almost time for his feeding. He was so good on the plane. Other people wanted to hold him. He is smiling a lot more and seems to be more awake than before. The only problem was during takeoff. I guess the cabin pressure was affecting his ears. They suggested I give him a bottle so that the sucking motion would relieve the pressure on his ears. It seemed to work.

"How was your trip? Were you able to spend some time with your sister?" Adam asked

"It was nice to see everyone including Lorraine and Pete. They came down and spent some time with us. They extend their holiday greetings to you. They thanked me for the lovely time they had at Crystal Cove and especially the tour you gave them. I met my sister's new boyfriend. He seems like a nice person. They would like to come up to Crystal Cove to visit during the summer. They were looking forward to their New Year's Eve cruise. Speaking of New Year's, do you have any plans? I thought we would have dinner together and watch the fireworks." Chris suggested

"I like that idea. I will bring a couple of bottles of wine from The Vineyard. They are the wines from last year's harvest. I stopped in at the winery while you were gone to attend their yearly harvest celebration. The two bottles of wine I picked up made this year's list of "Best Pacific Coast Wines." I cannot wait to sample the wine." Adam sounded excited knowing he will be welcoming the New Years with Chris and the baby.

CHAPTER 16

WELCOMING THE NEW YEAR

The day of New Year's Eve, Chris prepared full course dinner for two. She also made some appetizers for later to go with the wine that Adam will be bringing. Adam arrived just before 6 pm. The table setting for two complete with lavender flowers, candles, and a beautiful set of dishes awaited them. Chris just finished getting dressed and putting on her shoes when Adam arrived.

"Adam, can you please bring down a couple of wine glasses from the cupboard. I will be right out." Chris hollered from her bedroom.

"Sure. I am going to put the wine and the glasses in the fridge to keep them nice and chilled. Do you have any preference, white or red, to go with our dinner?" Adam asked

"It does not matter which one you open. Nowadays, either one will go with any dinner entrée. I am sure we will drink either white or red." She responded

When Chris came out, wearing a silky, floral, red dress that outlined her slim figure as she moved about. The dress accentuated the curves of her body. She looked stunning in her dress. Adam had not seen her in a dress before that night. He was mesmerized by what he saw he almost overfilled the glasses.

"Wow! You look gorgeous. Are you expecting someone else to show up or you have another date?" asked Adam

"Thank you for the compliment. Now, you are being silly. You are my only date unless you want to bow out from me. I just felt dressing up for the New Year. Do you think it is too much?" asked Chris

"No, not at all, I am fortunate to be your date for the evening and having a beautiful girl across the table from me, forgive me for staring," Adam stated

"Now, I know you are just flattering me, but again thank you for the generous compliment. It has been awhile since I have worn a dress. I have lost enough baby weight to fit on some of my dresses. Speaking of babies, he did not have a very good nap today because of all the noise from the firecrackers. He finally went to sleep, but with the on-going sound of the fireworks and firecrackers, he will likely be awakened several times tonight. Let us sit down and have our dinner before the baby wakes up." Chris stated

"May I pour you a glass of wine?" Adam asked

"Yes, please. I have to warn you about my low tolerance to alcohol. I will have to apologize in advance, if my behavior gets out of hand, just slap me a couple of times to wake me from silliness.

"Although I don't expect any bad behavior from you, I am not into slapping women, regardless of how silly they behave," Adam stated

"Yummm, this wine is good, not too dry, and not sweet at all. It is very smooth going down. You made an excellent choice for the wine. We have talked a lot about me. This time, let us talk about you." Chris gives her stamp of approval on the choice of wine

"What would you like to know about me?" Adam asked

"Well, whatever you want to share. For starters, why a good-looking man like you is still single? On the other hand, are you hiding a girlfriend or a wife somewhere? Where have you gone in your travels?" Chris wants to know more about Adam.

"Now, who is being generous with their compliments? I warn you, my story is not as interesting as your story, but it is special to me. Before coming here to Crystal Cove Island, I fell in love with someone who I consider the love of my life. We had the kind of love that only happens once in a lifetime if you get lucky to find it. I found it in her. I am waiting for that second chance to be with her again, for life this time." Adam's voice broke a couple of times as he was describing his story, feeling the loneliness of not being with her.

"Wow! It sounds like you are still in love with her. How long have you two been apart? Is she still around?" Chris listened to Adam's story intently.

"It seems like a lifetime ago. I am willing to wait for her to fall in love with me again. Yes, she is still around." Adam explained

"You and I seem to have a lot in common with our love story. I am in love with a man that I could never have again. Fortunately, you may have another chance at love and reunite once again. Does she know how deeply you feel and have you told her that you would wait until she is certain about her feelings?" Chris asked with a great deal of interest.

"She figured it out once before, I want her to figure it out, how to fall in love with me, again," Adam said

"Sometimes, it is not easy for us women to figure it out, unless we hear the words. You have heard the saying, "Men are from Mars and Women are from Venus." We do not process feelings and emotions the same way. I think you need to tell her how you feel." Chris gave him advice even though she felt envious of the woman.

"I plan to do that all in due time. I want to give her the space to figure it out, which I believe in my heart that she will." Adam sounded confident that it will happen.

"In a way, I think my life has been pre-determined by having my son to love. It is a gift from God to have a part of him with me forever, through our son. I hope he grows up to be like his father, kind, thoughtful, patient, loving man. I already know that he will be a very handsome young man. Of course, as his mother, I am a little biased. By the way, would you like some dessert? I know you are not a dessert guy, but I couldn't resist the choices of macadamia-coconut cheesecake or a flourless chocolate layer cake that were on display at the bakery shop for the New Year's celebration. It looked so decadent, sinful, and alluring; we just have to try it. Life is too short, so why not be daring once in a while? Would you like to indulge in some sinful desserts?" Chris changed the subject to lighten up the conversation.

"I have never heard anyone describe dessert as you just did. For someone like me who does not have a sweet tooth, I cannot wait to taste them. Before we have dessert, the music coming from the living room makes you want to get up and dance. Would you do me the honor of dancing with me?" Adam politely extended his hand to Chris.

Chris experienced a flash of memory of Mark at that moment. "I would like that. Just getting up from the table and dance is a wonderful idea." Chris placed her hand on Adam's extended hand.

Baby Ben started making noises by all the sounds coming from the fireworks outside. He began to cry so Chris went too looked in on him and bundled him up to bring him in the living room. Adam was already in the middle of the room, just waiting for Chris. Chris walked in with the baby as he extended both arms to dance with both of them. The baby seems to be enjoying the music. Then, the baby turned to Adam as if he wanted to climb up his chest. Adam noticed it and pulled him up to secure his hold on him. Chris put her arms around both of them and laid her head on Adam's chest as she watched her son rest his little head next to Adam's heart. Tears started flowing down her cheeks. She imagined this touching moment with the love of her life, Mark. Adam looked down at Chris and saw that she is crying quietly. He held her even closer, seemingly understanding precisely what she was thinking at that moment. To hide her emotions from Adam, she walked away and went to the kitchen to have a glass of wine. She wanted to be "numbed" from thinking about Mark. Adam wanted so badly to follow her and comfort her, but he held back until the time is right. The baby had fallen asleep, so Mark walked into the kitchen to ask Chris if he can put him down on his bed. They both went to the baby's room. Chris took a few minutes to tuck her baby in and lovingly just watching him sleep. There were a couple of hours left before the New Year. Adam came back out to the kitchen to pour himself a glass of wine before going to the living room. He stood in front of the fireplace, holding a glass of wine in one hand and the other hand resting on the mantel, seemingly in deep thoughts as he watched the wood burning in the fireplace.

"A penny for your thought, would you like to dance?" Chris asked as she opened her arms.

Adam gave her a big smile and walked up into her arms to dance. He did not say much, just held her close. He wrapped both his arms around her waist. In turn, she placed both her hands around his neck as they slow danced. It has been a long time since Chris felt a man's arms around her body. Her low tolerance for alcohol and a man's body so close to her; she felt her body wanting more. She started to kiss his face and eventually kissed him on the lips. He, too, wanted that woman's touch that he returned her kisses with more passion. Without thinking and pure instinct, he scooped her off her feet and carried her to the bedroom. She did not resist or stopped him. They stood in front of each other as they started to undress. She was having some problems with the zipper on her dress, so she asked Adam to help her. They both got under the covers, anticipating the most intimate moment when the baby started crying. Chris got up right away and threw on her silky robe to check on the baby. Adam laid there for a moment, then, after about fifteen minutes, he got up to put on his clothes. He went to get a glass of water and sat on the couch. Chris emerged from the baby's room and sat on the rocking chair.

"Adam, I am sorry about what happened tonight. It has been a long time since I felt a man's body next to mine. My low tolerance for alcohol heightens my natural response to your tender touches it made me want you. I lost my practical senses, caught in the moment. It is not fair to you what I did. Your friendship means a lot to me, and I do not want to lose that kind of friendship. However, if you do not want to speak to me again or continue to be my friend, I will understand." Chris was trying to explain her side.

"You are painting a picture of an innocent man in all of this. I am not exactly the saint that you make me out to be. I reacted like a normal man with the desires and wants when a beautiful woman such as you wants intimacy. My only disappointment is that it did not happen, no harm, no foul, saved by the baby." Adam tried to make light of things that almost happened.

They both felt somewhat awkward talking about what did not happen. They both sat quietly knowing that in a matter of minutes, the clock would be ringing in the New Year. When the clock struck midnight, the firecrackers, fireworks, horns, etc. that surrounded the neighborhood awakened the baby. With Chris's concurrence, Adam went in to get the baby as Chris served the dessert. All three of them welcomed the New Year by kissing the baby at the same time when the clock struck midnight. It must have been after 2:00 AM when Adam went home.

CHAPTER 17

DISCOVERING TRUE FEELINGS

After Adam spent New Year's with Chris, he thought a lot about their relationship. He cannot deny his strong feelings for her, not wanting to lose her. Right or wrong, he has to accept that she cannot move on with her life because she convinced herself to hold on to Mark's memory. In Chris' heart, she believes she cannot love another man knowing that Mark is very much alive in her mind. It is this mindset that Adam cannot compete with a man that exists in Chris' world. Until she recognizes her true feelings for Adam, he has no other choice but to put some distance between them. Understandably, Chris must have felt the same, not wanting to admit that she has feelings for Adam.

Chris took on a part-time job as an art teacher at a nearby elementary school. She asked Betty and Carla to watch over the baby for about 3 hours a day. They were delighted to have the baby at their home for a few hours. She did not need the money but needed some employment where she can use her other skills and interact with other adults. Also, Chris sees the benefit of having the baby see other faces, hear other voices and different surroundings, even if it just for a few hours.

At the same time, Adam got a job with a cable company, installing communication towers in the state of Washington, including the islands like Crystal Cove. The firm is home-based in Seattle where the training facilities are held and the main corporate office. Adam would be required to stay in Seattle during the week and goes home on weekends until he completed his training. The last day of training, he met his team and his team lead, Cynthia, a newly divorced woman, raising two boys in their teens and lives in Seattle. Her good looks at times get in the way of some men misbehaving through no encouragement from her. As the team lead, she was direct, precise and very professional with her team. Upfront, she told her crew to think of her as one of the men. It is against work policy that no love interest can be on the same team. It could be an automatic termination if this policy is not followed. Working closely with Adam as a new trainee, she would often talk to Adam about her sons and their issues because he listened and she trusted him. He gave good advice drawn from his own experiences as a rebellious teenager before joining the military. Their relationship remained strictly as co-workers. One Friday afternoon, Cynthia and Adam just pulled in front of his house. They have a big project on the other side of Crystal Cove to complete before Sunday night. They planned to work early mornings until dusk or as needed to complete the project on time. There were no rooms available at the Inn, so Adam offered his spare bedroom for the weekend. Chris happened to be coming home when she saw Adam with a woman entering his home. They did not see her coming from the opposite direction on her way to pick up the baby. She looked surprised and somewhat jealous that he was with another woman. She tried to put it out of her mind, but she could not let it go. For some strange reason, she felt a sense of betrayal, not understanding why she felt disappointed when there were no ties between them except good friendship.

Adam and Cynthia would have an early start, lasting until late in the evening. The next time she saw them was on Sunday afternoon. Not having seen them leave early in the morning and come back late at night, Chris assumed they were having a love-fest and never left the "love-nest." After about an hour, he came back without her. He saw Chris and the baby out on the porch, so he stopped in as he usually does. This time, Chris was acting cold and standoffish. He soon realized that she must have seen Cynthia but did not want to ask any questions. From her demeanor, she was definitely annoyed and bothered but pretended like there was anything wrong. Adam decided to play it up a bit and see how far he can take this 'jealousy' attitude. He said what he had to say and left. This went on for a couple of weeks, not talking to Adam.

He finally had enough of this 'cold fish' attitude. He also missed not seeing the baby. After he parked his car, he walked over to where Chris and the baby were playing just to say hello.

"Have you been trying to avoid me?" Adam asked her directly.

"No, not at all, I have been busy since I took on this part-time job. You seem to be the busy one, with your new woman." Chris said it with an attitude.

The tone of Chris' voice when she answered Adam sounded sarcastic unbecoming of the Chris he knows. In some ways, it was flattering to his male ego, but he wanted to end the cold attitude.

"Oh, you mean, Cynthia. She is my team lead and a coworker, not my 'new woman.' We had significant repairs on the other side of town to complete in a short time. There were no rooms available at the Inn at the time, so I offered her the guest room. She and other men from Seattle came to complete the work. We worked early in the morning until late at night to get it done. That is why I have not been around. Just so, you know, it is against the work policy to have any romantic interest within your team. It could result in immediate termination if found guilty. I just stopped in to see how you two are doing. My schedule has been erratic due to being new at my job. I am sorry for not being able to stop by sooner." In his mind, he felt something was happening between them, yet, he does not want to confront the matter in case he is wrong.

Chris felt terrible after Adam explained why he had not been around. He did not have to explain because they were just good friends. The snotty attitude made her feel even worst that she apologized.

"Adam, I am sorry, for my attitude. I just thought you had forgotten us, now, that you have a woman in your life." Chris apologized to Adam.

"She is my boss, not a 'person in my life. She is in no way looking for any romantic relationship, considering all the responsibilities on her plate. As the team leader, she knows the rules of engagement with team members." Adam stated the work policy.

"As my peace offering, would you like to have dinner with us? I just made some casserole, and it is about ready to be eaten." Chris meekly asked.

"That is the best offer yet, home cook meal. Having to work long hours, we ate mostly breakfast bars, snacks, and quick meals. It smells good. I just need to wash up. May I help you set up the table?" Adam agreed with no hesitation.

"Better yet, after you wash up could you hold the baby and I will set up the table? What would you like to drink? Would you like ice-tea, lemonade or a glass of wine?" Chris was delighted he accepted the peace offering.

Adam wanted to hold the baby since he stopped by. He missed the little guy. He came to him so quickly, surprisingly.

"I would like a glass of wine, please. How is it working out with Betty and Carla taking care of the baby?" asked Adam

"They are both such good babysitters, and they take excellent care of him. I am so fortunate to have such wonderful neighbors around me. They take the baby for walks and visit with other neighbors. He is happy when I see him." Chris tells Adam how she appreciates Betty and Carla.

"How do you like working at the elementary school? Is it what you expected?" Adam asked

"It has been great. The kids are well behaved and have good manners. The classes are small, perfect number of students per teachers, unlike the public schools in the big cities. My work hours are perfect. I would not want to be away from the baby any longer than that. I do have a small problem that I would like your honest opinion." Chris stated her small problem.

"Shoot, what is it?" Adam responded

"There is a new vice-principal who came from another school, temporarily staying at the Inn while looking for a place to live. He was from a private school in Vancouver, Washington. He was one of the people that interviewed me and hired me on the spot. He has been asking me to meet him at the Inn for a drink after school. I have told him about my son, and it would be difficult for me to find the time to go out." Chris stated.

"Is he hinting at wanting to move in with you?" Adam asked right away.

"No, I would not let anyone move in with us. He must be lonely not having anyone here on the island. I remember feeling alone when I first arrived until I met you all. Fortunately, I am surrounded by good neighbors." Chris explained

"What do you know about him? Maybe, he is married or with significant other back in Vancouver. Did he transfer here voluntarily or was he asked to leave?" Adam inquired.

"I am glad I talked to you about it, being that you are a good judge of character. Not too many people seem to know much about him. He has only been at school just before I was hired." Chris stated

"Do you want to go out with him or you just want to return the gratitude because he hired you?" Adam asked a direct question.

"I do not feel like I have to go out with him because he gave me the job. I can relate to what he is going through, remembering how isolated I felt not knowing anyone here, which changed when I met you all. I am running out of excuses for not wanting to go out with him." Chris stated.

"Why not let others go out with him before you do. That way you can find out more about him through others unless you are attracted to him and curious to find out what kind of a man he is." Adam said it with a sense of jealousy.

"You are probably right. I should find out more about him before I would even think about having a drink with him. I think I felt sorry for him." Chris said

"Do you recall the incident with Larry, when he tried to charm you to possibly get you drunk so that he can take advantage of you?" Adam brought up Larry's name, which surprised Chris. After he said Larry's name, he realized his error. Chris never mentioned Larry's name before.

"How did you know about Larry? I never told you about him. I make it a point of never mentioning his name." Chris sounded so sure she never uttered Larry's name in front of Adam.

"Yes, you must have talked about it once before. Otherwise, how would I have known his name? However, that is not important. We are talking about this new person. They all start out as a 'nice guy' to impress you. Then, their true motives are something else. Just be careful and not to be too trusting." Adam may have dodged a bullet, but he saw the puzzled look from Chris' face of not ever mentioning Larry's name in front of Adam. He knows he slipped, big time. In Chris' mind, she wondered how he would have known about the incident.

"It was not so long ago that you told me to learn to trust again.

Now, you are telling me something different. What changed?" Chris questioned Adam to get his perspective on how to handle the current situation with one of her colleagues at the school.

"I have gotten to know you more. I am sorry if I sound overly protective, but I just want you to be cautious. You asked for my opinion, perhaps, I said too much. Generally speaking, most women have the upper hand because they seem to have this "built-in" mechanism or radar that automatically goes into overdrive when it comes to romantic relationship. Am I right? On that note, I had better leave before I put my other foot in my mouth. Thank you for dinner. Can I help you with the dishes?" Adam wanted to avoid making more mistakes and walk away unscathed. He looked over at Chris and saw that she had a slight grin on her face, which was a good thing to see.

"No, I can manage a few dishes. Besides, you have to get up early in the morning. I do not have to go to work until after lunch. Good night, Adam." She bid him good night, feeling good about their conversation.

CHAPTER 18

TEARS, HOPE AND DEVOTION

Finally, Chris and the baby were about to experience their first summer weather on Crystal Cove Island. Other than occasional overcast in the morning, the rest of the day remained sunny and warm, mostly in the mid 70's. Flowers were in full bloom, fruits and vegetables grown on the island are plenty and the daylight hours are getting longer. The summer months bring out the tourist as well as the locals. Along the main roads and just about any day of the week you will find open marketplaces selling fruits, vegetables, freshly baked goods, canning products. Further down the road, there will be vendors selling arts & crafts and sometimes local wines. The one thing that is clearly visible is the smiling faces everywhere you go. The energy in the air is as bountiful as the happy smile coming from people whether they are locals or as a tourist.

The sun shining brightly through the sheer curtains in Chris' room woke her up. As she stretched her arms, she could not wait to start her day to take the baby out for a walk and check out the local farmer's market in her neighborhood. The first thing that Chris did was to check on the baby to see if he was awake. He was still sleeping. Chris was just looking at her son endearingly when she stroked his head. It felt warm. She immediately picked him up to hold him. The baby felt warm all over. She tried calling Adam, but he must have gone to work. Her other option was to call Betty or Carla to see if either one could drive them to the local hospital. As soon as they arrived in ER, they took the baby to the examination room when the doctor arrived. They checked the baby's vital signs and ran some preliminary tests to determine the situation. After they ran several tests, the doctors told Chris that the baby needed other tests that were not available at the local hospital in Crystal Cove. The baby's temperature continued to rise.

Time was of the essence; they will have to take the life-flight helicopter to Children's Hospital in Seattle.

Chris and the baby took the 20-minute helicopter ride to Seattle Children's Hospital. When they arrived at the hospital roof-top, several doctors and staffs met them. After several hours, the doctors determined that baby Benjamin has a blood disorder that he will need a bone marrow transplant from his parents or a perfect match. Chris cried profusely because the baby's father has passed away. She would be the only other parent left. They took her blood test and found out that she was not quite a match. The doctors asked if the father had any siblings that they can type within seventy-two hours. That is the extent of time needed to type and process the donor safely. The hospital went into an alert mode to expand the effort in finding a donor. Chris cannot believe what is happening. Her friends Tom, Marie and Sandy, came to the hospital. Chris could not calm down and required mild sedation to avoid any hysteria.

Adam finally arrived at the hospital. The moment Chris saw Adam; she tried to run up to speak to him. She was not making any sense. He tried to calm her down, but she continued to be agitated. They gave her more sedation to avoid hurting herself. Adam spoke to the doctors to get more information. Adam was gone for about 5 hours. No one knew where he went. It was the following morning when Adam came back. He told them that he had to go in to work in Seattle due to some power failure. Shortly, after Adam came back, a couple of doctors came to see Chris. She was just coming out of sedation. She started crying already, thinking that her baby was gone. She held on so tightly to Tom, who happened to be standing next to her.

"Ms. Jensen, I am Dr. Ahmed. I have some good news for you. We may have found a perfect donor for your son. We are currently processing the donor's blood getting it ready for the bone marrow transplant. This is the best match we found for your son. However, I have to be honest and straight with you. There is no guarantee that it will be a success. We would not know for another twenty-four hours if the baby accepts it or rejects it. It is a matter of a waiting game." Dr. Ahmed delivered the news.

"Who is the donor? Where did you find this person?" Chris was demanding to find out whom this person is.

"I am sorry, but the donor wants to be anonymous, and they have the right to remain anonymous in compliance with the HIPAA (Health Insurance Portability and Accountability Act) Law. By law, the confidentiality to remain private is highly guarded and tightly sealed. Only authorized personnel keep the legal papers in a vault accessible, not even the doctor has access to the document for everyone's protection. More importantly, they hope the transplant will work. They wish you both the very best and to hope you will meet someday." Dr. Ahmed explained.

"How is that even possible that I cannot find out anything about the donor? How will they find us?" Chris wants to thank the donor.

"Ms. Jensen, I understand your question about the donor. It is the HIPAA law that we must adhere to to protect individuals' confidentiality. The donor asked only for minimum information, such as changes to your name, address, phone number, and a nearest relative or friend not living with you. They will let you know if they would like to get in touch with you. I am sorry I cannot give you any more information on the donor unless he or she signs a release form." Dr. Ahmed re-assured Chis on the legality of being an anonymous donor. He went on to say, "For now, let us hope and pray that the baby will accept the transfusion."

"Doctor, I have to see my baby, please?" Chris was begging the doctors to see her baby.

"The baby will be brought to the staging area in about 20 minutes. He is being prepared for the bone-marrow transplant. He is heavily sedated." Dr. Ahmed said. He saw the desperate look of a mother, wanting to hold her baby.

"I just want to hold him as long as I can before the procedure." Chris wanted so badly to be with her baby.

"Okay, let us go see him for a few minutes. They just wheeled him into the staging area where we can see him." Dr. Ahmed approved the request after seeing the look of sadness in Chris' eyes.

Of course, everyone came too, but the doctor only authorized Chris in the staging area to hold her baby for a few minutes. They all could see the baby through a thick glass. She picked him up and kissed him. She held him so tenderly and whispered I love you. She could not stop crying. The nurse gestured that she has to take him now. She did not want to, but she kissed the baby before handing him back to the nurse. There were no dry eyes amongst her friends that have been watching from the other side of the glass. As Chris and one of the doctors came out, Adam was just on the other side of the door, waiting for Chris. He took Chris in his arms as she almost fell to her knees from worrying and exhaustion. They stayed in the waiting room, not saying much to one another as they waited for any updates on the baby. The bone-marrow transplant for babies takes about a couple of hours vs. an adult take four to six hours. However, it will take 24 hours to find out for sure if the procedure was successful. Chris just could not sit still or lay down. She decided to go to the chapel. Adam followed her there and sat beside her. They were the only people in the chapel.

"Adam, I cannot lose him. If God takes him, I want to go too. I have nothing to live for without my baby." Chris was serious with her statement.

He turned to hold her and said, "Ssshhh, do not talk that way. You have to be strong and think positively about the baby." Adam whispered in her ears.

They held each other for a long time, not saying very much. Marie entered the chapel to take Dr. Ahmed to update Chris.

"I just wanted to let you know that the transplant went smoothly. The critical time is within the next four hours. If the body accepts the transplant, the baby's temperature should start to come down. That would be our first milestone. Next, would be the baby's skin color. He should have some pink tint to him. He will probably be crying because he is hungry, wants mommy's milk. Then, we can safely say, we are on track for an excellent recovery. Those are the major milestones for your son." Dr. Ahmed stated.

As soon as the baby's temperature started to come down, Tom,

Marie, and Sandy left for the night. They planned to come back in the morning. They hugged and kissed Chris before they left. Only Chris and Adam were by themselves in the room together as they achieved each milestone. Twenty-four hours came and went. The baby survived the bone-marrow transplant and recovering in the ICU nursery. Both Adam and Chris could not stay away from the nursery. They just stood on the other side of an enclosed glass partitioned room to watch the baby. Chris refused to eat or sleep but just wanted to hold her baby so badly. The doctors convinced her to take a rest since she has been up more than twenty-four hours. They told her that she needed to be strong when the baby wakes up for his next feeding. She tried lying down, but she could not sleep. Adam sat by her side and just cradled her hoping that she can take a small nap. He rocked her just a little but maintained the stronghold as he continued to cradle her until she finally fell asleep. After about an hour, the nurse came in to get Chris to breastfeed the baby. She immediately went to the nursery. They sat her on the rocking chair as she fed baby Ben. She was so happy when the baby was actively taking in her milk. Adam was just on the other side of the partitioned window, watching Chris and the baby that nearly brought him to tears. Oh, how he wanted to tell her the truth.

Chris and the baby stayed in the hospital for ten more days, making their stay a total of 2 weeks. During that time, Adam was able to work in Seattle, so that he can be near them. He was in the hospital every night, never leaving Chris' side. The primary doctor who performed the transplant came in to give them the good news. The baby's recovery was going so well. After he examined the baby, he said he was, active, smiling a lot and playful. If he continues to progress in this manner, he may leave the hospital in a couple of days. Chris let out a big sigh of relief; she just buried her face in Adam's chest as she wept with excitement. Adam put his arms around her and just held her close and kissed her on the forehead to let her know how happy he was hearing the good news. Later that night, she found a quiet moment to write a compelling letter to the donor that saved her baby's life. She expressed how profoundly she felt as the mother of a child who received a precious gift of life from a kind stranger. She went on to say she hopes to meet them someday to thank them properly and to meet her son. She could never repay them for the gift of life they have given her. Enclosed was a check for $10,000 as a small token of her appreciation. As they were preparing to leave the hospital, Chris had one more thing to do before they depart. She has an appointment with the head surgeon that performed the transplant. She just stopped in to say goodbye and thank him for the miracle he has done. She handed him the letter to the donor and handed the check for $10,000 donation to the Children's Hospital. He hugged her and wished them the very best.

CHAPTER 19

THE POWER OF TRUE LOVE

The final service provided by the hospital was to take Chris and the baby to the Heli-pad location where their transportation to Crystal Cove awaits. As they approached the small airport in Crystal Cove, there was a crowd of people waving for them. Almost the entire neighborhood must have come to welcome them home. They had banners, "Welcome back, Chris and Baby Ben!" She was deeply touched and appreciative of the loving reception from the entire town. They were like rock stars given a warm welcome. As they landed, Betty and Carla were at the forefront of the crowd along with the local mayor, politicians, TV / Newspaper coverage, principal/teachers from Chris' school, and many people from her neighborhood, including Adam who was standing in the background. Chris did not expect such a crowd of well-wishers who came to welcome them home. She was looking for Adam, the man who never left her side. Adam stood in the back and waited for the crowd to show how much her neighbors loved them. They were like a celebrity as the local TV station covered their arrival. Adam could not wait any longer and walked up to Chris and the baby. He asked if he could hold the baby while the local TV reporter interviewed Chris. She obliged and handed the baby to Adam. She thanked the crowd for the welcoming reception. Betty and Carla invited all the well-wishers to come to Chris' house for sandwiches and refreshments. Chris was happy to be home. Adam drove them home as the crowd followed, forming a parade on display. The baby was asleep, so she put him down on his bed. She then came out to thank the people for the heartfelt welcome they received. The people stayed long enough to give Chris a welcome back hug. Betty and her sister prepared all the treats and refreshments. They stayed to clean up the kitchen and put away the food. Chris went to the kitchen where Betty and Carla were cleaning up. She hugged them both and started to cry, not knowing how to thank them for all the love and support they have given her. All three of them were crying with tears of happiness. They have become like a family to her. Adam was the last person to leave.

"Adam, can you stay awhile longer?" Chris asked

"Sure, do you need anything else?" Adam replied.

"I do not know where to start. Thanking you for all the things you have done for us since we arrived in Crystal Cove just is not enough. Your mere presence in our life and the continuous care, kindness, love, and support you have given my boy and I must be a gift from God. I could not have made it to the finish line during my baby's ordeal in the hospital without your strength to pull me through my dark moments. You were always by my side when I needed comforting, and you probably do not know it, but you have this calming effect on me. I am blessed to have experienced similar feelings once before, so I know the woman that you have been waiting for is a fortunate woman to have captured your heart of gold. With that said, you unknowingly made me want to be that woman. I hope and pray that I will find the kind of man like you someday. I realize now that there will come a time when I have to let go of the only love I have ever known, so that I can love that way again. Adam, you had better go. I have taken so much of your time." Chris opened her heart for the first time in a long time. She spoke genuinely from her heart.

"Chris, what are you saying? Are we in that awkward situation again where we cannot seem to go to the next level beyond friendship? What is it that you want?" Adam somewhat confused with what Chris is talking about. If only she knew, the woman he has been waiting for has been right in front of him all this time.

"Adam, there is only room for one woman in your heart, and that is already taken. I hope to find that happiness and have that kind of love again. I will cherish our friendship forever regardless of what happens to us." Chris replied.

Chris walked Adam to the door. In her heart, she did not want him to go. They stood in the doorway when Adam turned around to kiss her on the cheeks.

After their talk, Adam could not stop thinking about the statement Chris made about the other woman. He sensed that she would like to be that woman in Adam's life, but she could not take him away from her. How does he tell her what is in his heart?

It has been weeks since baby Ben was in the hospital. He was getting better and more animated and active as the days went by. Chris started giving him more solid food by adding cereal to his milk formula. She also made homemade baby food with the local organic fruits and vegetables available. He was sleeping longer at night and making more noises when he is awake. Chris received a letter from the donor. When she opened the letter, the check she wrote was included. She humbled herself upon receiving a precious gift of life for her baby. The letter simply stated that the money should be set aside towards the baby's college fund. They hope that when he grows up, he will be able to save another life. They are happy to hear that the baby is well and on the road to good health. They still hope to meet him in person, possibly on one of his birthdays.

Warm weather brings the people outdoors. Almost every afternoon when Adam gets home from work, he would see a playpen or a big blanket laid out on the grassy area just inside the white picket fence. He walked over and saw Chris and the baby rolling around the blanket, having a good time enjoying the warm sunshine. It was so inviting that Adam removed his shoes and joined them. The baby can crawl and likes being airborne when tossed up in the air. Chris and Adam sat across each other and tossed the baby back and forth. They played "London Bridge's falling down," with the baby in between them, mimicking falling down on the blanket. There was a moment when they were lying down that they locked eyes. Adam leaned into Chris and kissed her on the lips ever so lightly. She stood up right away, to avoid any further action from either one of them. She hurriedly went to the house to get a drink of water. Adam followed her inside, with the baby.

"Would you like something to drink? I have some fresh lemonade, ice tea, or soda." Chris asked.

"Yes, I would love some of your lemonade. It is always so refreshing, especially like today." Adam replied

"Lemonade is coming up, would you like some cookies, homemade by Betty? She brought it over earlier today." Chris offered some snacks to Adam.

"Sure, it is difficult to refuse whatever Betty makes. She is such a good baker; she had me spoiled when I first moved in the neighborhood." He said

"I am planning to celebrate the baby's first birthday, around Labor Day weekend. I was thinking of inviting the neighbors, my friends from the apartment complex and my students from my art class. What do you think?" She asked Adam.

"I think that is a great idea. A first birthday is an important event in a child's life. To be one-year-old, that is a major accomplishment." Adam agreed

"I cannot believe my little man is turning one. It just seems like yesterday that he was being born. He has gone through a lot that is why I want to celebrate his life. Did I tell you that in addition to donating to the hospital, I sent the donor a check for the same amount to thank them for the gift they have given me? I received a very nice reply back from the donor. The donor returned the check, directing the money towards his college fund. What a generous person, a stranger at that. On the note, they would like to meet him face to face, possibly on his birthday. It would be so special if the donor came to his first birthday." Chris told Adam the response she received from the donor.

"If you word it that way, he or she may want to meet your son on his first birthday. However, this person might ask to speak to you ahead of time to explain why they wanted to be anonymous. They may have a good reason for making the choice they made. You should suggest meeting at a common place, like the Crystal Cove Inn. I can come with you if you like." Adam gave Chris some suggestions.

"Yes, I would like you to go with me. I think meeting them first on neutral location before the party is a great idea. We would have an opportunity to meet face-to-face and properly thank them in private.

They may want to remain anonymous, after meeting us. There are only a few more weeks before his birthday. I had better start writing the letter." Chris agreed with Adam.

"Not to change the subject, I wanted to let you know ahead of time that next week you might see Cynthia in and out of my house. She is still training me on a variety of repairs that I might have to do alone." Adam wanted Chris to know about Cynthia.

"Why are you telling me all of this?" Chris interrupted Adam and sounded annoyed.

"It is important to me that you know the kind of man I am. I have been honest with you from the beginning, up to now. I do not like to play games that can hurt people, especially my heart. You have not mentioned anything about my kissing you earlier. Did you think it did not happen or if you ignore it, it will go away? Which is it?" Adam wanted an explanation.

"We know each other's story so well, and the mutual 'understanding' we have of being off-limits makes it difficult for me to answer your question. It is getting harder and harder to walk the fine line between friendship and a romantic relationship. You and I know we have had instances when we find ourselves in awkward situations, like right now, because we do not know how to label our feelings, such as the kiss earlier. Perhaps in my mind I have convinced myself that we could only be friends, yet, my heart tells me differently. I have to hold back my feelings for fear of being hurt, and you can go on to freely pursue the love you have been seeking. I have found that kind of love once, thinking that it is enough to sustain me forever, but lately, that thought is slowly fading. I do not want to admit what is happening between us is real because it means I am letting go the love of a man that will never love me back. My heart wants to find that love again. That is the truth of where I am in my life." Chris admits.

"Since we are being honest about our feelings, I have had to question your actions. I do not know if you are just being flirtatious with me because you know you could get away with it. There are times when you are being 'daring' knowing that I cannot do anything about it because of the 'understanding' that we have about each other – being off limits. The 'unspoken' relationship we have; I have to look at you differently.

Otherwise, you will not be standing there and me, over here. I would hold you in my arms and make passionate love to you, but I know I cannot do that. I do not know how you feel about me or how you see me. I am afraid to make a move simply because I do not want to take the risk of losing you. Here we are again, in an awkward situation. We have been here several times. We just do not know what to do about it." Adam was extremely honest about his feelings.

"This is the feeling of 'letting go' that I am talking about. It would be so easy for me to jump into your arms and tell you all the things you want to hear. There is that little voice telling me I am letting go of the memories I have been holding on to for a long time. Also, I know you are in love with a woman that will be in your life soon, so I cannot put myself in the middle of your relationship." Chris was trying to convince herself why she cannot fall in love with Adam.

"Is this your way of convincing yourself you are faithful to a man that does not exist on this earth? If he were the man you say he is, he would set you free to follow your heart to find that love that you had with him. No one in his or her right mind can compete with a 'ghost' of the past. Do not settle for half the life. You have the right to have a full life, not half ass." Adam was passionate about his point.

"I have heard those exact words once before. This is like 'déjà vu' all over again." Chris has had this similar conversation with Mark, using the same words. Reflecting back to when she met Adam, there have been so many serendipitous instances that only happened between her and Mark, not with Adam.

"I better leave before I forget where I am. Think about what we talked about today. I will not bring up this matter again. You know where to find me when you figure out what this is. I ask only for one thing, not to come to me unless you are sure you want me in your life completely. Do not worry; I will help you with the birthday celebration. I will put on a happy face for the sake of the baby. You have my word." Mark clearly stated his honest feelings.

Chris could not sleep that night. She tried to process the discussion she had with Adam earlier. Why does he tug at her heartstring so much? Why are her feelings toward Adam getting stronger as her memories of Mark starting to fade? Could she be falling in love with Adam, but do not want to admit it or is she just fantasizing about Adam? Mark did tell her once to follow her heart to find that happiness she deserves.

As the daylight hours began to get shorter and shorter, it is an indication that the end of summer draws near. It would be a matter of a few weeks before baby Benjamin would be celebrating his first birthday on Labor Day weekend. Chris wants to plan a birthday celebration, inviting the neighborhood, her friends from the apartment complex, and the donor to come to the baby's first birthday. It would be a major event in his life.

Adam kept his distance without being obvious. He would only stop over when Chris and the baby are outside. He kept his visits and conversations at a minimum. The more he stayed away, Chris was missing him terribly, and her feelings were growing stronger.

CHAPTER 20

REVELATION FINAL CHAPTER

Several days passed when Chris received the letter she has been waiting for. It was a reply from the donor, willing to meet first before coming to the party. She wanted to tell Adam about the good news, so she waited until he got home, but he did not come home that day. The next day, he came home early. Chris saw him pulling into his driveway. She waved at him to come over. He walked up to the fence to tell her he had been working all night and needed a shower. He will be over after he takes a shower.

"You look all fresh, nice and clean. I waited all night, but you did not come home." Chris told Adam.

"I was in Seattle all day and night to repair several towers due to a windstorm. I have not slept since yesterday. Is everything all right?" Adam was concerned.

"Yes, everything is all right, but we can talk later. You look so tired. Would you like me to fix you something to eat?" Chris asked.

"No, thanks, but I would like something to drink, whatever you have is fine. I am more tired than I am hungry. Let me just sit here for a minute. Where is the baby?" Adam asked.

"He is napping at the moment. Let me fix you something to drink. I wanted to tell you that I received a very nice reply from the donor. They are coming to the birthday party, but want to get together at the Inn the day before the party. I am excited to meet the donor finally." Chris said as she was coming back to the living room when she found Adam asleep on the couch. He probably did not hear a word she said. She stared at him shortly and bent down to kiss his face, then, his lips. She whispered in his ear, "I love you." There was a slight chill in the living room. Chris took out a lap blanket to cover Adam, who was completely out. He slept through the entire afternoon until he woke up at around seven pm. Chris was in the other room changing the baby after his bath. Adam came into the room to see the baby.

"Hey, you finally woke up. Are you hungry now? I did not want to wake you to have dinner." Chris said

"Gosh, I did not realize how tired I was. I am sorry; you were saying something before I dozed off. What were you saying?" Adam was apologetic.

"It can wait until tomorrow. You had better have something to eat before you go home. There is a pot roast and mashed potatoes still warm. What would you like to drink? Would you hold the baby, while I fix you a plate?" Chris offered Adam something to eat before he went home.

"Sure, I would love to hold the baby, especially after a bath. I am so hungry just smelling that pot roast. You can talk to me while I am eating." Adam excited to hold the baby while Chris fixed his dinner.

"I received a very nice reply from the donor. The donor agreed to meet before coming to the party. He/she will be staying at the Inn." Chris sounded excited.

"Did you still want me to come along with you or this person just wants to meet with you?" Adam asked

"They did not say to come alone. I would still like you to go with me if you are available. Otherwise, I think I will be okay to go by myself." Chris responded.

"What if I just go with you to the Inn and keep my distance. This person might want privacy when they talk to you." Adam suggested

The day finally arrived for Chris to meet face-to-face with the donor. She has been nervous all day. Betty and Carla volunteered to watch the baby when she meets the donor. Adam went along with her to the Inn, to give her some support. When they arrived, there was a note for Chris to go to suite 4E. The suite number was familiar to her. She was in that same suite with Mark. As she walked down the hallways, flashes of memories came to her. She hesitated for a moment until she knocked on the door and found it opened.

"Hello…anyone here?" Chris implored.

"Come in, please." A man answered

When Chris came around the door, she saw Adam. It caught her by surprise, so she asked, "What are you doing here? Do you know the donor?"

"Yes, I do. I know him well." Adam said in a very serious voice

"How do you know the donor? Why did you not tell me you know the donor? Is this some prank? If it is, it is not funny. Where is this person?" Chris asked

Adam hesitated for a moment and said, "I am the donor. Let me explain."

Chris interrupted and started to back up headed towards the door. She said, "No, this cannot be. Get me out of here…"

Adam went after her and put his arms around her before he said, "Sssshhh, Chris, it's Mark, but let me explain." He tried to restrain her, but she fainted and started to fall. He caught her and scooped her off her feet to lay her down on the bed. He got some ice cubes and towels to apply cold compress on her forehead. After a few minutes, she started to come around slowly. Still a little dazed, she tried to get up, but he was at her side to hold her down. She tried to fight him off. He held her down to begin explaining what has happened.

"Let me go," Chris commanded.

"Not until I explain to you what this is about. Can you give me just five minutes to talk to you? If you want to leave, I will let you go." He said. Chris lay still on the bed.

"Chris, I need you to trust me one last time. I am sorry to have done this to you, but it is for our own good. I will set you up so that we can talk. I have been waiting for this day, to be with you and our son, no more secrets or disguises. We have a bright future as I promised. We can now live a normal life, but I have to remain as Adam because my external being had to change my identity, including my fingerprints and my voice inflication, to protect us and complete the mission. My inner person, my DNA, remained intact that is why I was able to be the perfect donor when our son needed the bone marrow transplant. I had to remain anonymous until it was safe to come out. One more thing, I told you early on that you have my heart and soul. I can assure you; I did not change. I never stopped loving you, and I am more in love with you now, this moment. As Adam, I wanted you to fall in love with me, again. I do not know if you ever got there. Therefore, I need to ask you a question. How do you feel about Adam?

"How do I know who you say you are? Just telling me that you are Mark doesn't make it so." Chris questioned the man in front of her.

"That is a fair question. Let me answer you. Do you remember the first day you met me? You stared at my eyes as if you recognized me, did you? Did you feel an instant connection with me, because I felt it right away? There were little things I purposely did as Mark that you would recognize such as not liking dessert, how I took my tea with honey, I used the words "half-ass" when we talked about our relationship. How would have I known about Larry? The biggest connection was with our son. He immediately took to me as if he knew all along that he was my flesh and blood. Have you asked yourself why you have such strong feelings for me? When I told you about the woman I have been waiting for, it has always been you." He assured her that the reasons he just stated were not coincidences but facts. He eased up in holding her down, hoping that she remembered what they had experienced together.

"I am going to ask you again how you feel about Adam." He asked again.

"Mark, Adam, I do not know what to call you. I am having a hard time making sense out of all this. Mark will always be the love of my life, who gave me a son. Adam renewed my faith in being able to fall in love, yet, I could not admit it to him. It would be like betraying my love for Mark. Adam gave my son a second chance at life when he needed the bone-marrow transplant. The first time Adam held my son, they bonded so naturally, as if my son instinctively knew his father. I was amazed at seeing the genuine love and devotion happening between my baby and a stranger. Looking back, Mark and Adam have many uncanny qualities that I have come to love that conventional logic could not explain in a million years how that was even possible. Still, I defied my feelings for Adam because I would be disloyal to Mark's memory, the love of my life. The last thing Adam told me was not to come to him until I knew for sure what I feel in my heart. This is probably the most difficult thing I have to do, that is to say, *"goodbye, Mark, farewell my love..."*

At that moment, tears were streaming down her face, imagining seeing Mark fade away and the sight of Adam becoming clearer as he stood in front of her with his open arms. Chris stood up and looked into Adam's eyes then let out a smile. She reached for his hands to pull him towards her. He embraced her right away as they kissed so lovingly.

"Adam, I love you with all my heart." The sad tears became happy tears as she continued to hold Adam ever so tightly.

"I have wanted to hear those words from you, my love. I never stopped loving you. I love you with every fiber of my being. My faith in God that He blessed us with a child shielded me from all the dangers that I faced during the year we were apart. Our destiny brought us together again and made our love even stronger than ever before. When we were in the chapel at the hospital, I wanted to tell you the truth about the donor, but I also wanted you to fall in love with me as Adam. I picked this suite because you and I have made unforgettable memories here. Now, I want us to go home, be with our son so that we can plan our future together. That piece of paper we signed at that small church near the lighthouse was an authentic, legal document. You and I have been husband and wife since we declared our love before God. Nonetheless, I would like us to go back to that same place to have our wedding. Our son will bear witness to his parents love for one another. Chris, will you marry me, again?" Adam was so loving as his blue eyes started to well up.

"Yes, I will marry you. I love you so much..." Chris had tears of happiness as she responded to Adam's proposal.

It took only a couple of weeks to put their wedding together. They both decided to go back to the small church, where it all started. The elderly/ priest happened to be there the day they visited the chapel. They asked him if he would be there for their wedding day. He was delighted and honored to preside over their wedding. They also requested Lorraine, Pete, Betty, and Carla to be their witnesses. Tom and Marie walked her down the aisle as Sandy held baby Ben and both served as the bridesmaid and best man. Chris wore a beautiful ivory-lace dress and Adam wore a business suit. They all walked down the short aisle to the altar. Both, Chris and Adam wrote and recited their heartfelt vows. They reached for their son Ben just before the priest declared them as "man, wife, and son." The wedding party emerged from the small chapel as the sun was setting down behind the mountains of Christmas pine trees and the subtle scent of salty ocean water from Crystal Cove Bay provided the perfect backdrop to a serendipitous union between Adam and Chris, with their son Ben and their circle of friends who witnessed their once in a lifetime love story as they fulfilled their destiny...

...the end...

ABOUT THE AUTHOR

As a first-time author this is my first book. What was I thinking that prompted me to write, you ask? It was in my "bucket list" to do when I retire. Having immigrated to this beautiful country just before becoming a teenager, I had to learn English quickly. From then on, I have always been fascinated by learning new words and listening to people who speak and write English well. As a novice writer, you are surrounded by lots of words, so Thesaurus is my new friend.

My husband and I retired about seven years ago. We looked forward to our retirement years, so called our "golden years." I haven't figured out what part is considered "golden." It is hard to believe we just celebrated our 40th wedding anniversary on a cruise to Alaska. Perhaps, another ten more years with my wonderful and terrific husband will be our golden anniversary. Ah, there is the golden years. Happy reading!

Printed in the United States
By Bookmasters